DEMONS
ARE
FOREVER
THE REALM SERIES

AE JONES

AE JONES: DEMONS ARE FOREVER

Publisher: Gabby Reads Publishing LLC

Cover Designer: theillustratedauthor.com

Editor: demonfordetails.com

PRINT

ISBN-13: 978-1-941871-24-9

AUTHOR'S NOTE

When I started writing the Realm books, I quickly realized that some of the scenes would need to crossover into the other books. Misha, Aleksei and Sergei's stories are interlocking in time—it's a close family, after all—so as you're reading the first three books, you'll probably notice some scenes you've read before...but from a very different perspective. Amazing what you can learn from a new point of view.

I originally planned on only writing a trilogy, but I couldn't get this family out of my mind. So two more books were born! Marrick first appears as Naya's loyal best friend in *Demons Are A Girl's Best Friend* and I wanted to tell this honorable demon's story.

And Boris...this over-the-top father and clan leader has a special place in my heart. How could I not give him a happy ever after?

Prepare for some fun with this outrageous but loving family!

Kelly –
Thank you so much for becoming a member of our family (even if you had to marry my brother to do it). I'm sure you have probably looked at us over the years and thought more than once, "What did I get myself into?" But you're ours now—there is no escape! Thanks for accepting us, warts and all!

CHAPTER 1

Sergei Chesnokov was a demon without purpose. A pathetic admission, especially for someone two hundred forty-five years old, but true nonetheless.

The bell sounded, announcing that the plane had taxied to the gate and passengers could leave their seats, and the people around him leapt into action. Always the same—everyone trying to wrestle with bags that were too big and should never have been in the overhead to begin with, then jockeying for position to rush off the plane to their newest adventure, only to have to wait for their connecting flight or ride.

Sergei used to be like them, traveling throughout the world for the past century to experience everything it had to offer, and using his camera to capture it. So much anticipation. Hell, he had been one of the first to cross the ocean on a commercial flight. There was something about being the first that appealed to him. Maybe being the third son played into it. Growing up, he had never been the first to do anything...except disappoint his father.

"Is everything okay, sir?"

The plane was empty, the flight attendant looking at him with concern. "Yes. I'm fine. I'm not in a rush, so I decided to let everyone else get off first."

She smiled. "It is a bit much, isn't it?"

Sergei pulled his backpack out from under the seat in front of him and stood. "Yes." He grabbed his appropriately-sized duffel from the overhead as well.

She walked with him to the front of the plane. "Is Chicago your home?"

Chicago. He'd forgotten where he was for a moment. Nonstop traveling did that. "No. I'm not home. Have a good day."

The teeming crowd of people had him stopping in the middle of the terminal to get his bearings. He hadn't been in the States for a while now, and it always took a few days to acclimate. Next step was to grab something to eat and then figure out where he wanted to go next.

Sergei pulled his phone out and switched out of airplane mode. In seconds, it beeped, telling him he had a voice mail. He frowned at the name—Irina, his grandmother. She insisted that he call her on Sundays if he was in an area that actually had cell phone service.

The call came in an hour ago—five pm on a Tuesday. His stomach twisted. Something had to be wrong.

Sergei hurried over to the wall, dropped his duffel at his feet, hit play, and listened.

"Sergei, you need to come home. Aleksei is in grave danger. Call the following number and talk to Kyle. She'll pick you up at the airport and explain everything. Please, Grandson. Your family needs you."

Sergei's chest tightened. What kind of message was that? What had happened to his brother?

He called his grandmother's cell, but it went to voice mail. Then he listened to her message again and wrote down the number for this Kyle person before rushing to the ticket counter. Luckily only one person stood in front of him. He studied the flight screens while he waited. A flight to Cleveland left in less than an hour. Stepping up to the counter, he booked a seat on the plane even though the ticket agent said he would have to run to make it.

Ticket in hand, he ran toward the gate and yelled for them to stop before they closed the door. He clambered onto the plane, stuffed his duffel into an overhead, and dialed the number his grandmother had given him. The person answered on the second ring.

"Sergei?"

"How—"

"Irina gave me your number before she left. Where are you?"

"I'm in Chicago, and just got on a plane for Cleveland, so I should be there in an hour."

"Good. I'll be at arrivals waiting for you. I'll be in a black van."

"What's going on, Kyle? Where's my grandmother?"

"Your family is trying to help Aleksei."

Sergei let out a breath at the use of present tense. "So he's not dead."

"No. I'll explain everything to you as soon as I can, but it would be better to do it in person."

Sergei gripped the phone tighter and opened his mouth to argue.

A flight attendant stopped beside him. "I'm sorry, sir. You'll have to turn off your phone now."

"I'll call you when I land, Kyle." Sergei hung up the phone and flipped it into airplane mode as the plane taxied down the runway.

He leaned against the headrest and rubbed his hands on his jeans.

"Are you okay, son?"

He hadn't been paying attention to anyone when he boarded, and he turned to look at the older human female next to him who'd made the comment.

"I'm fine."

"Are you afraid to fly?"

He shook his head. "No."

"Are you traveling for work?"

He wanted to ignore her questions, but he had been taught to respect elders, even though he was older than she was by at least a hundred years. "I'm visiting my family."

"Ah. Families are both wonderful and stressful. I hope your trip home is a happy one." She picked up the book in her lap and thankfully began to read.

Home. He didn't have a real home anymore. And now the family he had for all intents and purposes abandoned was in trouble. His grandmother had been telling him for a while now to come home, but he always made excuses. Now he didn't know what awaited him.

He hadn't spoken to either of his brothers in a long time. He had little in common with his older brother, Misha, and the last conversation he had with Aleksei had ended in an argument. What if those were the last words they would ever speak to each other?

Sergei ran his hands over his face. He had a lot to make up for. He just hoped he wasn't too late.

An hour later Sergei tightened the grip on his duffel as he emerged from baggage claim to look for his ride. He searched for a few minutes until a black van shot across two lanes of traffic and came to a screeching halt in front of him.

The passenger window rolled down and a young woman with a black pageboy studied him for a moment. "Sergei?"

"Yes."

"I'm Kyle. Get in."

He yanked open the back door and threw his bags on the floor as he took a seat. The van pulled away before he completely shut the door.

The male driving was a vampire who apparently fancied himself a race car driver, or, since he narrowly missed clipping the car next to him, maybe a demolition derby driver.

"Damnation, Jean Luc. That was close!"

"Sorry, *ma petite*."

She turned to Sergei. "I'm Kyle, and this is Jean Luc. We work with your brother Misha at the Bureau of Supernatural Relations."

The BSR was the supernatural version of a detective agency. They solved crimes and hid the existence of supernaturals from humans, who might be a little upset to learn that demons, vampires, and shifters were very real. But why would the BSR be involved in whatever happened to his brother?

"What type of trouble is Aleksei in?" he asked.

"What do you know about Aleksei's job?" Kyle replied.

Sergei thought for a moment. His grandmother had told him something about Aleksei taking on a new role, and how proud she was of him. After that, Sergei hadn't registered much of what she was saying. His stomach cramped. He was a selfish prick. "Not much, other than it is a new job to help demons."

Kyle narrowed her eyes at him. Apparently she didn't find his answer acceptable. "Aleksei is heading up the newly formed Bureau of Demon Immigration. He's helping relocate demons to earth from the demon realm."

Sergei sat up straighter. "The demon realm is a prison. Why would we bring them here?"

Kyle frowned. "Because the realm demons have been trapped there for a millennium. They're being punished for a war that took place before they were even born. The demon race needs to stop segregating themselves. Two groups have already successfully migrated here, but many in the realm don't trust us. Aleksei went there to meet with various clan leaders and find a way to build trust."

Of course his brother did. "Damn it. Tell me what happened."

"The Kelmar clan has taken him hostage because they want to do an exchange. We have one of their clan under arrest, and they want him back."

"And where are Father, Misha, and Grandmother?"

"They're in the realm."

"What! Father let Grandmother go to the realm?"

"Your father didn't *let* her do anything. I know it's been a while since you've been home, but your grandmother has a mind of her own."

That she did. "Where was the portal guard when Aleksei was taken?" The supernatural equivalent of prison guards, the portal guard was supposed to keep the realm demons from killing each other, and also from coming to earth.

"Naya, the leader of the portal guards was taken hostage first. Aleksei traded himself for her."

Of course he did. It seemed Aleksei was still the paragon of honor in the family. "So let's exchange the Kelmar for Aleksei and be done with it."

Again with the narrowing of her eyes. He was definitely on this female's shit list.

"The Kelmar prisoner is an Abstatholm. Which means he can form portals to move between earth and the realm."

Yep, if she felt the need to explain an Abstatholm to him as if he was a youngster, he wasn't just on her shit list, he was at the top of it.

"He attacked the Shamat compound and tried to kidnap two small children and take them to the realm. We won't be releasing him."

A realm demon attacked their clan compound? "Was anyone hurt?"

"Minor injuries only. Which is why Aleksei went to the realm. He wanted to convince the realm demons that earth is a viable option."

"So what's the plan, then? How are we going to free Aleksei?"

"We're going to show the realm that Aleksei is a demon of action, not lies. Your family went to help, and Irina hopes that you will go and stand alongside them."

He pressed his hands against his jeans to calm himself down. His brain was on overload, and guilt surged through him. He heard her underlying message, and couldn't blame her for doubting whether he would have come at all if not for Grandmother's plea.

It also didn't help knowing that even though he'd shown up, he truly couldn't be of much help. He wondered if his grandmother told Kyle the truth about him. That he was an aberration—a demon without powers, born to the leader of the Shamat clan, no less. But this wasn't about him, so he pushed his insecurities away.

"When do I go to the realm?"

CHAPTER 2

Lela stood just outside the firelight so her clan members wouldn't see her. Until recently, she had always been proud to call herself Kelmar. But now she wondered if her clan was on the cusp of losing everything due to fear and ignorance. Ever since the immigration was announced, her father had become distrustful to the point of paranoia. Since he was the Kelmar clan leader, his distrust impacted everyone.

When her clan members Joran and Tarem began filling her father's head with lies, her concern increased. She tried several times to tell her father the two demons were going to destroy his clan's chance to go to earth, but he wouldn't listen. And now Tarem had recruited demons outside their clan—a Lagfel and a Majock—to spread the lies throughout the realm.

Two days ago, Lela almost convinced her father to give the immigration a chance, until Tarem informed them that Joran had been captured by the earthers for no reason other than him being from the realm. Having known Joran her entire life, Lela was certain there was more to the story, but there was no convincing her father of anything now.

And when Tarem showed up with the unconscious portal guard to bargain for Joran, she worried all was lost. Now? Now the earther had exchanged himself for the guard, her hopes for a better future had been destroyed.

Lela watched the earther, who was tied to a tree. He had tan-colored skin and green eyes. She had never seen anyone like him before. According to the murmurs she overheard, he was in his human form. Unlike realm demons, demons on earth used two forms—human and demon—while realm demons stayed in their demon form. Her orange skin and yellow eyes would probably scare the humans on earth. Not that it mattered anymore. She would never go to earth now. Her clan had ruined everything.

She carried a blanket over to the earther, who sat far enough away from the fire that he would be cold as night set in. She dropped the blanket by him. He reached toward her, and she flinched away. But he wasn't trying to touch her, instead grabbing the blanket and pulling it toward him.

"I'm sorry. I didn't mean to scare you. Thank you."

She backed away from him, nodding, and went to her hut. But before she could enter her home, Tarem blocked the door.

"Lela. What were you doing with the earther?"

"I gave him a blanket. If we plan to exchange him for Joran, he should be healthy."

Tarem scowled. "I don't care if he's healthy or not. Stay away from him."

She tried to step around him, but he grabbed her arm, and she bit back a groan as energy ripped through her and ran like fire down her arm and into his hand. He let her go after a moment, and she staggered before rushing into her hut and slamming the door.

She sank to the floor and wrapped her arms around her knees. She imagined shrinking down until no one paid attention to her anymore. Until no one stole from her anymore.

In the past few weeks Tarem had gotten greedy, not leaving her enough time to recuperate before extracting more and more of her energy.

One day he would take too much.

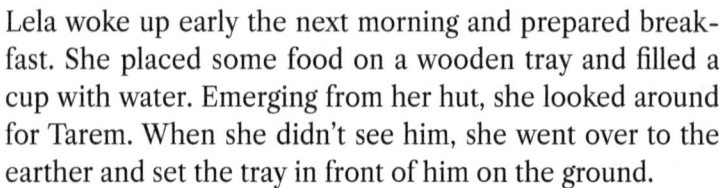

Lela woke up early the next morning and prepared breakfast. She placed some food on a wooden tray and filled a cup with water. Emerging from her hut, she looked around for Tarem. When she didn't see him, she went over to the earther and set the tray in front of him on the ground.

He smiled. "Thank you for the food. I'm Aleksei. What's your name?"

She glanced back over her shoulder to see if anyone was watching her. "Lela."

"Have you seen Saboll this morning?" he asked.

"My father is out for his morning walk."

His eyes tightened on her at the word "father." "I would like to talk to him."

She shrugged. "You can talk, but he might not be willing to listen."

"I'm here to help the clan."

She tilted her head and stared at him. "I thought you were here because you're tied up."

Aleksei chuckled. "Very true. But I think we can find a way to work things out. If your clan doesn't want to come to earth, you don't have to."

She shook her head. "Most of us don't want to stay here."

"Does your father know?"

"No—"

"What are you two talking about?" Tarem strode toward them.

"Nothing, Tarem."

He stormed up and kicked the wooden tray, spilling Aleksei's food on the ground and grabbing her arm. A scream of pain burst out of her before she could hold it back.

Aleksei struggled to get to his feet. "Stop! You're hurting her!"

After another agonizing moment, Tarem let her go, and her legs collapsed. Aleksei reached for her with his bound hands, but Tarem shot a burst of energy into Aleksei's chest, doubling him over.

"You don't touch her," Tarem snarled, as lightning jumped between his fingers.

Lela sat up and blocked Aleksei's body with her own. "You can't kill him. Father is expecting to trade him for Joran."

Tarem closed his fist and the lightning disappeared. "I'm watching you," he growled before stalking away.

Aleksei crawled over to her. "Are you okay? What did he do to you?"

"Touch hurts me. It drains my energy."

His eyes widened. "You're like a conduit for power."

She scrunched her face at his description.

"It means the other demons are able to increase their powers by taking your energy."

"Yes. Which is why Tarem is so powerful. But it doesn't last long, and then he comes back for more."

"But it's making you sick. He's taking too much."

She blinked away tears. "He doesn't care. It's only about being the strongest. Soon I will have nothing left."

"You mean he'll kill you." He glanced over to where Tarem stood with the Lagfel and Majock demons. "Why don't you tell your father?"

She shook her head and stood. "I can't."

"Then I'll tell him."

"No! Tarem will kill you, and if you die, they'll shut the realm off for good, and never let any of us leave."

Aleksei opened his mouth to argue, but she cut him off.

"Please. I can handle this for now. If you ever speak to my father, you need to tell him about the immigration. That is what matters."

Aleksei nodded, even though his eyes told her a different story. She would not let him sacrifice himself for her. Not if it meant her people would be trapped in the realm forever. Her life wasn't worth that.

CHAPTER 3

Sergei walked behind Kyle and Jean Luc into the Shamat meeting hall. A small human woman with blond hair and intense green eyes stood at a long table packing clothes into duffel bags.

"Sergei, this is Callie. She works for the demon immigration bureau." Kyle turned to Callie and kept on talking. "Where are we with the original five?"

"They should be here any minute." She smiled at Sergei. "The first group we brought to earth contained five realm demons. One from each clan. Aleksei felt that each clan needed to be represented in the initial relocation."

"Majock, Kelmar, Lagfel, Dragan, and Palthat, in case you need a refresher on the realm clans."

Sergei scowled at Kyle. "I know the realm clans."

Callie spoke. "We also have a representative from each clan who was part of the demon trafficking on their way as well. They're willing to reveal the truth of their experiences—the slavery, the threats and punishments—to stop the lies being spread in the realm."

Sergei gaped at them. "Demon trafficking?"

"What do you and Irina talk about on the phone each week?" Kyle sighed. "Never mind. Since we don't have a lot of time, here's the abbreviated version of what's happened. Abstatholm were bringing realm demons to earth and selling them as indentured servants. We found out about it, put a stop to it, and established the bureau that Aleksei runs to bring demons to earth legally." She smiled. "How was that?"

Before he could respond, the door opened, a number of demons entered the room, and Kyle went over to greet them.

Callie shot him a sympathetic look. "Sorry if this is over-whelming, but we don't have a lot of time to explain things. Time moves much faster in the realm than here, and we need to get everyone there ASAP."

Sergei set his bags down. "What should I take with me to the realm?"

"Clothes for a couple days. Nothing electronic. Our technology doesn't work in the realm."

Sergei pulled out a pair of jeans and some shirts and stuffed them into his backpack, then rezipped his duffel, leaving his camera bag inside. "Can you put this somewhere safe?"

Callie nodded. "Absolutely. I'll lock it in the office."

Across the room Kyle stood still for a moment with her eyes closed, rubbing a crystal around her neck.

"What is she doing?"

"Talking telepathically to Naya, the portal guard leader. They should be opening a portal to the realm any minute now. Are you ready?"

Ready? He literally clamped his teeth together to stop himself from laughing at the ridiculous situation. Realm demons, demon trafficking, time changes, and his brother being held captive...he was nowhere near ready. And it was nobody's fault but his own.

The far wall shimmered like a waterfall, and light burst outward before an enormous Pavel demon strode through the portal. Purple skin stood out against his black jump-suit—and was that armor?

Kyle clapped her hands together and addressed the group. "If you haven't met him before, this is Marrick. He's a portal guard, and he'll escort you to the realm. Marrick, I've got the original five, plus a demon from each clan who was part of the demon trafficking will be coming with you as well."

Sergei cleared his throat. "And I'm Sergei."

The Pavel nodded. "Excellent. Let's go."

Callie waved her hands to get their attention. "Everyone please grab a duffel bag to take with you to distribute to the clans."

Sergei grabbed a bag and walked to the portal. Yep, he was far from ready.

When he stepped through the wavy wall, it felt like he was trying to gulp air through a straw, but after a couple of moments, the portal spit him out into a world that looked like earth, but wasn't. They emerged in a clearing with trees surrounding them, and the air felt heavier, as if dust floated around them.

As the rest of the demons stepped into the realm, they changed back to their demon forms, their skin displaying an array of colors—orange, blue with black stripes, green with brown marks, gray, and finally light blue—for Kelmar, Majock, Dragan, Lagfel, and Palthat respectively. If Kyle was here, she would have probably pointed each one out to him. He might not have seen any of these clans in the flesh before, but he learned about the realm clans as a child.

Marrick faced them. "We'll walk for a couple of miles before we reach a portal to the in-between, where we'll meet with Naya and the rest of the portal guards to explain the plan."

The portal guard led the way, with the realm demons walking two by two like a supernatural version of Noah's ark. Marrick beckoned for Sergei to walk up front with him.

"You look like someone slapped you across the face."

Sergei grinned at his bluntness. "I feel like someone slapped me across the face. I was called home to find out my entire family is in the realm trying to free Aleksei from the Kelmar holding him captive. I didn't even know he was working to bring the realm demons to earth."

"That is a lot," Marrick said. "But Aleksei is a good leader. After the Shamat compound was attacked, he came to the realm to show the clans that earth is a safe place for them. He already convinced the Palthat, Dragan, and Lagfel clan leaders to give him and earth a chance."

"Until the Kelmar grabbed him."

Marrick frowned. "Naya was captured, and Aleksei exchanged himself for her. Naya is furious at him for doing that."

"Why did he? I mean, wouldn't it have made more sense for him to negotiate with the Kelmar for her release instead?"

"Aleksei was afraid they would hurt her. And he believes that if he spends time with the Kelmar leader, he can convince him to let him go."

"But you're not as certain."

"I have confidence that your brother could convince the leader if he wasn't also dealing with other demons who are trying to sabotage the immigration. And Naya is not willing to take a chance with Aleksei's life. Which is why we're continuing to carry out his plans. He promised the clans that he would allow them to meet and talk with the demons who have already been part of the immigration. He also promised to start providing supplies to those still living in the realm."

Marrick gestured to the duffel in Sergei's hand. "This will serve as a gesture of goodwill with the other clans. If we can get them on our side, they'll stand in opposition to the Kelmar leader."

"Smart plan," Sergei said.

"Yes. Naya is a smart female."

Sergei walked for a few moments in silence before Marrick spoke again. "You look like you have more questions."

"As a child, I learned about the demon wars and the five demon clans being sent to the realm, but I don't know much about the portal guard and the in-between."

Marrick replied, "The portal guard originated from the twelve demon clans that still live on earth. My ancestors were Pavel, and they volunteered to watch over the realm to keep the clans from coming to earth."

"So you've never lived on earth?" Sergei asked.

"No. I was born in the in-between. The in-between is where the portal guard lives. It's a space between earth and the realm. When we're on patrol, we jump through a portal from the in-between to the realm. All guards can move between both. Naya and I also have the ability to jump to earth as well."

"Like the Abstatholm."

"Yes. And they've been causing quite a bit of trouble. Spreading lies about what earth is like, apparently wanting to cause a rebellion, and they were succeeding until Aleksei came here."

"And now they're trying to make an example of him." Damn his brother. If Aleksei were a selfish bastard, he wouldn't be in this mess.

Marrick came to a stop and spoke to the group. "It's time to jump to the in-between. We'll arrive close to the guard village."

Again with the walking through pudding before they emerged into a large field. Marrick pointed to the left, where huts could be seen in the distance. "We'll be there in a few minutes."

They hiked in silence as Sergei attempted to absorb everything Marrick had told him. He was so out of touch with the demon world and his family. A family he was about to see for the first time in two years.

Outside the huts, a group of guards stood clustered around a table. Sitting at the table was a female Pavel with long black hair and purple skin, and next to her sat his grandmother.

The group looked over at them as they walked into the village.

"Sergei!" Irina called out as she jumped up and rushed over, throwing her arms around him. He bent down and hugged her.

He let her go and straightened. From the look on both Misha and Boris's faces, they had no idea Irina had called him.

His brother Misha grabbed him in an awkward hug before Sergei stepped back and acknowledged his father with a nod.

"How did you find out what happened?" his father asked.

"I called him, Boris," Irina said. "We need our whole family here."

Boris cleared his throat. "Thank you for coming."

Sergei swallowed down the awkwardness that threatened to choke him. His own father felt the need to thank him for showing up.

Was it too late to make things right with his family?

CHAPTER 4

The time had come. Sergei took a deep breath as he studied those around him. Naya led the group to confront the Kelmar. Not only was Sergei's family a part of this group, along with the realm demons Marrick brought back from earth to visit, but the clan leaders and many of the members from the four other realm clans had also joined the crowd.

Irina grabbed Sergei's hand and walked next to him. "I'm so glad you came, Sergei. I wasn't sure if you were in an area where you would get the message."

"That's a nice way of excusing my general lack of responsiveness."

She frowned. "I am an honest demon, Grandson. If I wanted to scold you, I wouldn't be passive-aggressive about it."

He squeezed her hand. "I know. I guess I'm scolding myself for a lot of things right now."

"I'm not going to tell you to stop if it means you're going to visit home more frequently." She winked at him.

"Yes ma'am."

After a while they passed through foothills until they came to red crystals embedded in the ground. According to Naya, the Kelmars' village was built by the crystal caves, so they had to be close. A shout ahead of them alerted the Kelmar clan, who emerged from a group of huts to gather in the village center. A large Kelmar stood in the forefront. Sergei assumed it was the leader Naya had told them about, by the name of Saboll.

Standing behind the leader were a Lagfel and a Majock. They must be the demons who'd been traveling throughout the realm spreading lies. Sergei quickly looked around for Aleksei, and spotted his brother standing off to the side. Other than being tied to a tree, he didn't appear to be injured.

Naya strode toward Saboll with her staff in hand. She came to a stop in front of him and thumped the tip of her staff into the earth.

Saboll glanced over the crowd behind Naya, as if looking for someone. "Where is Joran?"

"He will not be returned to you," Naya said. "He is facing sentencing for his attacks on earth, as the Majock and Lagfel behind you should be doing as well."

The Kelmar leader straightened and puffed out his chest. "So you are willingly sacrificing the earther. As the head of my clan, I claim blood rite for the loss of my clansman."

"And as the head of my clan, I claim right of refusal," Boris called out.

"No!" Aleksei shouted struggling with his bindings.

"You are the head of your clan?" Saboll asked Boris.

"Yes. As head, I can determine who will face you in the rite."

"As can I." Saboll gestured to a Kelmar standing to his left.

Naya spoke. "Before we start killing each other, I demand to speak in Aleksei's defense. But first, untie him so he can be part of this."

Saboll nodded, and a Kelmar untied Aleksei and brought him over to stand next to the Kelmar clan leader.

Naya continued. "Aleksei and his family have brought two groups of demons to earth. This is not a lie. The immigrants are doing well on earth. The other clan leaders asked for proof of this claim, and, as Aleksei promised them, we have brought proof in the form of the first five immigrants, who are standing behind me. They came back here willingly to tell the clans about their experiences on earth."

A tall Kelmar demon stepped up beside Naya.

Saboll spoke. "Kall? You have returned."

Kall nodded. "I came to tell you that earth is everything the realm is not. Our clans have a chance to thrive on earth. If we kill the demon leader responsible for helping us, nothing will be the same. Why would the earth demons be willing to trust us after that?"

The Dragan clan leader spoke up. "Listen to him, Saboll. If you don't want to leave the realm, you don't have to, but it doesn't give you the right to destroy the opportunity for others to leave. We have spent a millennium trapped here. Now we have the freedom to choose."

Saboll shook his head. "The Abstatholm—"

"Have lied to you," Naya said. "I don't know why they're spreading these stories. It could be fear. Even though many want to go to earth, the idea of leaving what we know is terrifying."

She straightened even more, and continued. "Or maybe they want to control the immigration on their terms. Before the official relocations, clan members were sent to earth by the Abstatholm, and we now know they forced those realm demons to work as slaves for them, threatening their families in the realm if they did not obey.

"Now that demons are able to go to earth without their help, it has taken away their ability to control and manipulate." Naya gestured behind her. "I have brought back several of those who were promised a better life by the Abstatholm, who will tell you what happened to them.

"It was the earthers who freed them from their slavery. Not the other way around."

The Lagfel and Majock standing behind Saboll ran toward Naya.

"No!" Grandmother yelled, flicking her wrist and using her telekinesis to lift the two demons off the ground, leaving them to dangle in the air, their legs kicking.

The large Kelmar next to Saboll pushed his way through the crowd toward a Kelmar female standing on the outskirts.

"Don't touch her!" Aleksei yelled before tackling the Kelmar as the female scurried backward.

Aleksei convulsed as the Kelmar's energy slammed into him. Sergei ran to help Aleksei, but before he could reach him, Misha shouted, and the Kelmar shot into the air and then slammed back down on the ground, hard.

Holy Fates, had Misha just used telekinesis? Boris ran over and hammered his fist into the Kelmar's face, knocking him out.

"What is the meaning of this?" Saboll bellowed.

As Aleksei struggled to sit up, Sergei jogged over and held out his hand to help him. Aleksei grabbed his hand, and Sergei pulled him up, and stood beside him.

"He has been draining Lela of her power. He's killing her," Aleksei said.

Saboll turned to the female. "Why didn't you tell me?"

"He threatened you, Father. Said he would kill you and take over the clan if I told you the truth."

Saboll reached for her, and she flinched. "Oh, my child. I should be the one to protect you, not the other way around. I have failed you." He looked around at the gathered crowd. "I have failed all of you. I have let my own fear cloud my judgment. It was much easier to believe what my clan members were telling me than risk sending us to a new world." He blew out a harsh breath. "What do we do now?"

Aleksei nodded to Naya.

She spoke. "Now we sit down and discuss next steps."

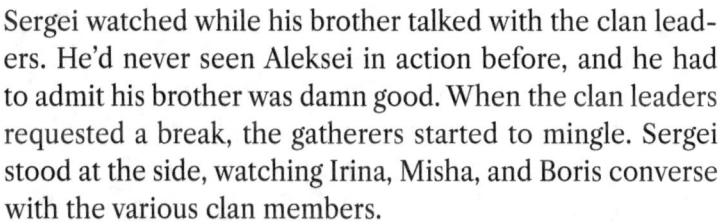

Sergei watched while his brother talked with the clan leaders. He'd never seen Aleksei in action before, and he had to admit his brother was damn good. When the clan leaders requested a break, the gatherers started to mingle. Sergei stood at the side, watching Irina, Misha, and Boris converse with the various clan members.

There was excitement in the air, as if something momentous had occurred. And hadn't it? Sergei studied the crowd until he caught sight of the female Aleksei saved earlier. She also stood on the outskirts watching.

Sergei turned in time to see Aleksei come over and stop beside him.

"It's good to see you again, brother. Thank you for coming."

"I'm glad you're okay," Sergei said. "I didn't know what to expect here."

"It is a lot to take in, and you got thrown into the deep end without any preparation."

"If Naya's plan hadn't worked, I'm not sure what I could've done to help."

Aleksei sighed and glanced away from his brother for a moment. "I actually think you *can* help. I want you to meet Lela."

Sergei followed his gaze. "The Kelmar female? She's terrified. Why do you think meeting a strange male would be helpful right now?"

"She needs to know not everyone will try to steal her powers. She needs a protector from the rest of the demons who will be surrounding her for the next few days."

"And how can I keep her safe? I wouldn't be able to stop anyone from touching her."

"You don't give yourself enough credit. I think she needs to feel safe with one person who can't steal from her."

Sergei frowned. "Because I'm a null."

Aleksei scowled at the word. "Sergei, you have always said your lack of powers is a disadvantage, but now, in this instance, it is exactly what is needed to help a female who has been abused. Are you willing to help her for a few days? And are you okay with me telling her about you?"

Sergei hesitated. Did he want that? But if he wasn't willing to help somehow, then why had he come here in the first place? "Yes."

Aleksei threw his arm around his shoulder, surprising him.

"Excellent. Let me check with her first."

Sergei watched him walk away. Aleksei never stayed in one place for long. He was a force that would help every one of these demons in every way he could. Leave it to his brother to find a way to use Sergei's lack of powers to everyone's advantage.

CHAPTER 5

Lela watched the milling crowd. Her father had tried to convince her to go to her hut, but she couldn't miss this. The five clans were actually working together toward a common goal. Her clan had not ruined their chances to go to earth.

When she saw Aleksei coming toward her, she smiled.

"Lela, how are you feeling?"

"Better." Maybe not physically, but emotionally she was exuberant. "Thank you for protecting me earlier."

"Of course." Aleksei answered as if it was a common occurrence. He looked around at the crowd. "I'm hoping these conversations will help the immigrations move more quickly and smoothly."

"I'm just happy my father is seeing reason now."

"Your father is unsure of the future. Fear is a powerful motivator."

She was well aware of how fear could control thoughts and actions. "I know."

"My family is here to learn as well." He started to point them out. "That is my father, Boris."

"You look like him, except for your eyes."

"Yes. And that's my grandmother, Irina."

"She is an amazing warrior. Was she going to stand up for you during the rite?"

"If she had her way, yes. Although my father would have had something to say about that. The male standing next to her is my brother, Misha, and over there is my younger brother, Sergei."

She looked over at the male standing away from the crowd. He was tall like Aleksei, but with dark blond hair. She couldn't tell if his eye color was green like Aleksei, or maybe light blue like Aleksei's father and older brother.

Aleksei continued. "I was wondering if I could introduce you to him? He knows nothing about the realm, and I thought he could sit here with you so you can explain things to him."

She fisted her pants leg. "I...why me?"

"Because he's standing over there by himself, and you're sitting here by yourself." Aleksei knelt down to be eye level with her. "Sergei feels like he is an outsider most of the time. If I tell you something about him, can I trust you to keep his secret?"

She nodded.

"Sergei has never developed powers. So seeing this world is a bit overwhelming to him. I thought it would be good to let you sit with him. And I also thought it would be nice for you to spend time with someone who won't try to steal your powers."

Her eyes widened as she looked over at Aleksei's brother. "Really? He can't hurt me?"

"He can't. You have my word."

She took a deep breath. "I would like to meet him."

Aleksei smiled and then beckoned to Sergei. "Wonderful."

Sergei came over and sat next to her on the ground, so thankfully he wasn't towering over her.

"Lela, this is Sergei. As you can see, I got both the looks and the brains in the family."

Lela chuckled. "And modesty."

Aleksei laughed. "Exactly!" He turned to his brother. "At the rate things are going with the clan discussions, I think we might be at it for a couple of days. And so you two aren't bored while we're talking politics, I thought Lela could tell you about the realm, and you can tell her about earth. Sergei has traveled all over earth. He will have plenty of stories to tell you."

Lela looked at Sergei, and swallowed again before dropping her gaze to the ground.

He had brown eyes with a hint of gold. So pretty, and yet she couldn't get herself to look back up at him.

Someone called Aleksei's name.

"Appears that they want to resume the discussion. I need to go join them."

He strode away, and Lela's stomach dropped. What should she talk about? "I'm sorry," she blurted, finally looking up at Sergei.

He gazed back at her with his golden brown eyes. "For what?"

"For what happened to Aleksei."

"Did you capture Naya? Did you convince Aleksei to trade himself for her?"

"No. I tried to tell my father not to keep the portal guard, and then Aleksei walked right into the village and demanded her release."

"Then you have nothing to apologize for." He watched his brother in intense conversation with the other clan leaders. "And I can imagine him doing exactly that."

Lela smiled. "He is a good male. After what my father and Tarem did to him, he could have stopped the immigration."

"Aleksei is all about honor and doing what's right."

She stared at him for a moment. "Why do you say that like it's a bad thing?"

His mouth turned up on the right side in a lopsided grin. "Thanks for calling me out on that."

"Calling you out?"

"It means not letting me get away with something. Honor and duty are good things. Some come by it naturally, others struggle with it."

She pondered his reply for a moment. "Then I would say there is more satisfaction for those who succeed after struggling, correct?"

His eyes narrowed on her briefly, and she held her breath, fearful she had said something wrong.

"You have an interesting way of looking at things."

It was time to move the conversation in another direction. "Tell me about your grandmother. She is a powerful female."

He gave her another lopsided grin. "Yes she is, and she's not afraid to let you know it. She holds everyone in our clan accountable. Even though my father is the leader, Grandmother is not someone you want to cross."

"And what about your other brother?"

"Misha is my oldest brother. He works on earth to keep humans from finding out the truth about the supernatural."

"So will he become clan leader one day?"

"Clan leader succession doesn't go to the oldest. It goes to the one with the strongest powers. Aleksei is slotted to take over the clan when my father steps down, except..." He stopped talking.

"Except what?" she asked.

"Nothing."

Had she said something wrong? "Aleksei told me you do not have any powers."

Sergei frowned before nodding.

She sighed. "What a blessing that must be."

Sergei felt like he had been hit in the gut with a baseball bat. When she asked him about his lack of powers, he prepared himself for the awkward pause, followed by The Pity Speech. He'd experienced it many times, but for her to think it was a blessing? What had this female suffered to make her think that?

She was a small female, with dark red hair that hung to her shoulders, light orange skin, and beautiful yellow eyes. Eyes that had dark circles under them. Between the stress of the last few days and these bastards violating her, no wonder she looked like she was ready to fall over.

"I'm sorry you've been hurt. They had no right to take from you that way."

Her cheeks darkened to a burnt orange. "No, they didn't."

"Can I ask you about your power?"

She stiffened and he held up his hand. "Never mind, we don't have to talk about it."

She shook her head. "No, that's okay. What would you like to know?"

"When did you realize you could give others your energy?"

"When I had lived thirteen summers, my father hugged me, and I felt energy push from me into him. He staggered back, and for the next few hours, the strength of his powers increased. He said it was like energy bubbled under his skin, and he had to use it."

"At first, he told me to keep it a secret. He didn't want anyone to take advantage of me. But it is too hard to keep that kind of secret, and I couldn't control the energy if I accidentally touched someone. My father has learned to block it, but anyone else..." She shrugged.

"So you avoid touching people."

"Yes. And then Tarem started touching me. At first he would accidentally brush up against me, but in the past few weeks he has simply taken."

Sergei clenched his fists. That SOB needed his ass handed to him. But Lela had already experienced enough violence. She didn't need to see him going caveman right now.

"You can't control the release?"

She shook her head before looking away from him.

"That's okay." He was in no place to judge her lack of control.

A rumbling in the crowd drew Sergei's attention to the clan leaders. They were all standing.

Aleksei jumped up onto a log and called to the crowd. "We're done for today, so there's time for you all to return to your villages before it gets dark. I'll be meeting tomorrow with the clan leaders in the Lagfel village to continue plans for the immigration, as well as ways to make life here better. Thank you for believing in me, in us. I am humbled by your trust, and will work hard to keep it."

They stood as the other clan members started to move around. Lela cowered away from the crowd as people moved toward her, and she stumbled.

Sergei grabbed her arm to steady her.

She jerked away and spun wide-eyed to face him.

He held his hands palms out to calm her. "I'm so sorry, I didn't mean to touch you."

She looked down at her arm and then at his hand. "Do it again."

"What?"

She held out her arm. "Touch me."

He slowly extended his hand and laid a finger on her forearm. He looked up at her and she nodded. He placed his whole hand on her arm.

She blinked, her eyes glistening. "It's true. You can't hurt me."

He swallowed. He couldn't remember even one time in his life when he'd been happy to be powerless.

Until now.

CHAPTER 6

Lela strolled around the busy Lagfel village. She wondered if Sergei would be there today as well. Aleksei was deep in discussion with a group of Lagfel clan members. When he saw her, he excused himself and joined her.

"I'm glad to see you. I was hoping you'd come with your father today."

"He doesn't want me to be too far away from him right now."

"Understandable. How are you feeling?"

"Better." And she was, even if it was only a little bit.

"I've brought a healer from earth to help some of the clan members who may be ailing. Would you meet with her?"

Lela bit her bottom lip, hesitating.

"She won't hurt you, Lela. She simply wants to help if she can."

"Okay."

He smiled. Lela had a feeling that Aleksei got his way most of the time. He led her over to a hut and knocked on the door, and a voice called out to enter. Aleksei motioned for her to go inside. "I'll come find you later to see how things go."

Lela's heartbeat increased as she entered the hut. A tall female was standing in the middle of the room. Even in human form, she was beautiful. Her hair reminded Lela of the light yellow field flowers that grew in the spring, her eyes were blue, and her skin was a light tan color. This was the healer?

"Hello Lela. I'm Sabrina. Aleksei asked me to come to the realm and help out for a while."

"And you think you can help me?"

"I would like to examine you if I may."

Lela shook her head. "I can't be touched."

Sabrina nodded. "Aleksei told me about your powers. I should be able to touch you without draining you."

"Are you powerless like Sergei?"

Sabrina looked surprised.

Had Lela said something she shouldn't have?

Sabrina gave her a small smile. "No. I'm a Succubus demon."

Lela gasped before scrambling away from her.

"Your reaction tells me you know what a Succubus demon can do."

Lela's heart pounded. "You drain energy from beings, demon or not."

Sabrina eyes tightened. "I can do that, yes. And that's the reason why I should not be a danger to you. I had to learn at a young age not to take energy from humans and supernaturals. I can control my power. I only take energy when the person gives me permission. I think I could help teach you how to block your powers as well."

"I don't know."

Sabrina sat down on a chair in the middle of the room, and Lela's tension lessened now the demon wasn't standing over her.

"What if I examine you without touching you? I can hold my hands above you and sense your energy flow. I often do that with my patients when I'm trying to determine what's wrong. Would you be willing to try that?"

Lela hesitated.

"I promise not to touch you."

"Then yes, you may."

When Sabrina smiled, her beauty astounded Lela.

"I'll stay seated, and you come closer to me when you're ready."

Lela took a step toward her and then another and another, until she stopped in front of her.

"Okay. I'm going to lift my hands, but I won't touch you."

Sabrina held her hands in front of Lela's chest and closed her eyes for a few moments. She then lifted her arms so her hands were above Lela's head. Lela locked her legs to stop herself from backing away.

"You're doing very well, Lela. Just a few seconds more." Sabrina dropped her hands. "Okay. I sense that your energy has been depleted. You are probably really tired, and you might even feel sick to your stomach."

"Yes."

"It's similar to a condition on earth called anemia. I'm going to give you some medicine called vitamins to help build up your strength again. We want to avoid allowing anyone to take energy from you for several weeks. I'm going to be here for a while, checking on other realm demons who might not be feeling well, so if you're willing, I would like to teach you how to control your power while I'm here."

Was it even possible? "I'd like that."

"Excellent." Sabrina stood and went over to a table with several boxes of supplies. She pulled out three bottles and placed them on the table. She opened one and pulled out a tiny white object. "This is a pill. Swallow one pill from each bottle every morning with a glass of water. Take the pills after you've eaten your breakfast." She picked up the bottles and placed them in a small bag. "Do you have any questions?"

"Earlier you said you don't take someone's energy without permission. Why would someone willingly give you their power?"

"You have only experienced people taking your energy without permission. They have violated your trust and stolen something from you. For Succubi, the exchange of energy is normally during sex. It can be quite pleasurable for both parties."

Lela could feel her cheeks heat. She had never had sex before. Never even been kissed. How could she, when she couldn't bear to have someone touching her?

"Would you like to stay with me today? I've been having difficulty getting other clan members to visit me. Maybe if they see you're willing to work with me, they will let me help them as well."

"Yes," Lela said. "But I think it would make sense to sit outside the hut and invite others over to meet you. It was scary to come in here, not knowing what to expect."

Sabrina beamed at her. "Great idea! We'll set chairs outside and then, if necessary, I'll bring some of them inside for their examinations."

Within minutes, they were both sitting outside the hut watching the Lagfel clan members milling around as the various clan leaders arrived.

Lela waved at an elder female, beckoning her closer. She introduced Sabrina to the elder, and explained what the healer was doing here. Who better than an elder in the village to bring those in need to Sabrina?

The elder left with a gleam in her eye, and Sabrina grinned. "You handled that very well. You gave her a sense of purpose. Now she'll bring the clan members to see me."

"Yes. I've learned by watching my father over the years. It is important to make people feel they are needed. They're more accepting that way."

"Yes, they are."

Lela narrowed her eyes at her. "But then I'm not telling you something you don't already know. You did the same thing to me a few minutes ago."

Sabrina laughed. "Yes, I did." She stood as the elder walked back toward them with another clan member in tow. "I think our day is about to get busy."

Lela breathed deeply and happily as warmth bloomed in her chest. When was the last time she had a purpose?

<hr />

Sergei walked along the field outside the portal guard village in the in-between. And then he jerked to a stop. He was in another *world*. Holy crap. He indulged his mini-freak-out until he heard someone call his name.

Misha jogged toward him. "What are you doing out here?"

"Getting some air."

Misha came to a stop next to him. "I'd believe that if it didn't feel like we're breathing in dust all the time we're here. I think you're avoiding Father. If that's the case, you can rest easy. Marrick is escorting him to the Lagfel camp right now. He's going to help Aleksei with the talks."

Sergei started walking again, and Misha fell in step next to him.

Sergei wondered how Lela was doing today. Aleksei had mentioned that he was going to have the doctor who arrived last night spend time with her. He hoped she would feel better soon. He thought back to her look of wonder when he laid his hand on her arm yesterday. How hard to live a life physically isolated from others.

"How have you been, Sergei?"

"Oh, no. The better question is how have *you* been? We're not talking about me right now. Not when I saw you pick up a demon with your mind yesterday and slam him to the ground. Considering the fact that the last time I saw you, that was not one of your powers, you owe me an explanation of how you developed telekinesis at this point in your life."

Misha grimaced and shrugged. "I didn't."

He stopped and turned to Misha. "I saw you—"

Misha held up his hand. "I'm not denying my telekinesis. I've been telekinetic since I developed my powers as a teen. The rest of the family found out a couple of weeks ago."

Sergei gaped at him. "Why would you hide them?"

"It's complicated."

"Are you kidding me? What the hell!"

Misha's eyes softened. "Sergei—"

"Don't! Don't say another damn word. I don't need your pity, Misha. I might not have powers, but I have ears that work. I've heard it all over the years. *Poor Sergei, the null. No powers. It's a good thing he's not an only child. His brothers can pick up the slack.* Do you know what I would have given to have any power at all? And you have powers that you don't even use? The Fates are vengeful, that's for sure."

He backed away from Misha before his brother could say anything else or pull him in for a pity hug. "I'm going for a walk. Alone." He strode away across the field before he said anything else he couldn't take back. How could his brother hide who he was? Why would he?

Anger surged through him like a wave from his head all the way down to his feet. His brother had been lying to them all along. And as much as Sergei could be blamed for abandoning his family, he hadn't lied to them about something as fundamental as his powers, or lack thereof. The anger threatened to burst through his skin again as he started a slow jog in the direction of the lake Marrick told them about.

He came to a stop next to the large body of water. The water lapped lightly against the shore as he sat down and leaned against a tree. He wasn't sure how much time passed before he heard footfalls behind him, and he looked back to see the portal guard leader, Naya, standing there.

"Did Misha send you out here to see if I threw myself in the lake? No worries. I know how to swim."

"It's not your swimming I was worried about. Do you know how to avoid celebaras?"

"Celebaras?"

"It's a combination of what you would call an octopus and crocodile on earth. It could eat you in a couple bites."

Sergei looked out over the calm lake. "Really?"

"No. I made it up."

He whipped his head around to look at her.

Her eyes sparkled. "Glad I got your attention."

"You're a comedian?"

"Sometimes, if I need to be."

"You're a female of many talents. If it hadn't been for you, I don't know what would have happened to Aleksei."

She sat down next to him. "I was the reason he was being held captive to begin with. The honorable fool exchanged himself for me."

Sergei chuckled. "That's a good description of him. It sounds like you know him pretty well."

"Yes. He's happy you're here."

"He told you that?"

"He didn't have to. I could see it in his face when he saw you. He told me you used to be close."

"Really? And when did all this sharing happen?"

Naya's eyes tightened on him. "You have a lot of anger, Sergei. I don't know all the reasons behind it, but I'm sure being in the realm isn't helping matters, nor is finding out about Misha's telekinesis."

"Not scared to speak your mind, I see," Sergei said.

"On earth a lot of pretty words are used to avoid the truth. Here in the realm, honesty is necessary, or demons get hurt. I am blunt."

Sergei turned back to the lake and stared at the water.

"You aren't the only one impacted by Misha's revelation," Naya said.

Aleksei. He couldn't imagine what he thought of Misha's powers. Aleksei had been groomed as the heir apparent since he threw his first fireball. "It sounds like you're pretty close to my brother."

"I would protect Aleksei with my life." Naya stood. "I'm on my way to the Lagfel village. Would you like to come along, or do you prefer to stay here feeling sorry for yourself?"

Sergei barked out a laugh. "You are blunt."

"Yes I am. You will get used to me...or not."

He stood. She was right. It was time to suck it up and help ensure the work Aleksei was doing here actually came to fruition.

Family drama could wait.

CHAPTER 7

Sergei ambled around the village. The Lagfel were a sea of faces in varying shades of gray. Excitement buzzed in the air. Earlier Sergei had passed Aleksei and their father sitting with the clan leaders, including Lela's father. However, Sergei had not seen Lela yet. Didn't she come with her father today?

There was a small crowd standing outside a hut. As Sergei approached, he saw the doctor from earth talking to a Lagfel male, and Lela was standing beside her. She was actually smiling at something the male said, and Sergei was surprised to see how a simple smile could light up her face.

After he watched for a few minutes, she looked in his direction and smiled even more brightly. He walked toward them, but stayed back so he wouldn't interrupt the doctor's examination. The crowd thinned out after a while, and Lela beckoned, inviting him over.

"Sergei. It's good to see you again."

"You're helping out Dr. Miller today?" Sergei asked.

"Yes. Sabrina has examined several clan members. She plans to go to all the villages to do the same thing."

"Lela's been a great help. She's helped alleviate some of their fears." Sabrina glanced between the two of them. "Why don't you take a short break and show Sergei the village?"

"Are you sure?" Lela asked.

"Absolutely. I can handle things on my own for a while."

As they headed away from the crowd, Lela led him around a cluster of huts for a bit before leading him to the edge of the village to stand looking out at the foothills that rolled gently in front of them.

"Thank you for spending time with me," she said.

He shrugged. "I should be saying that to you. Thanks for showing me your world. I'm glad to see you interacting with other demons."

Her eyebrows rose slightly, and he rushed on.

"I just mean that..." *Hell.* What did he mean, exactly?

"If we're going to make this work between the realm and earth, we have to be willing to do things we're scared of. I'm still afraid someone will steal my powers, whether on purpose or accidentally, but I want to make it better here."

"Do you want to stay in the realm?" Sergei asked.

Lela shook her head. "No. I want to go to earth, but before I leave, I still want to make it better here for those who wish to stay behind."

Damn. Spending time with her made him feel more than a little selfish. "Was Sabrina able to help you?"

"Yes. She's having me take things called vitamins? She said I need to build my strength back up." She bit her lip as if to stop the next thing she was going to say.

"What is it?"

"Sabrina thinks she can teach me how to control my powers. How to stop people from stealing from me."

"That's great. Why don't you look happy?"

"I am a little...scared."

Sergei turned to her. "That's understandable. But it's also exciting, too. Imagine not being afraid of someone's touch."

Lela's smile lit up her face this time. "That would be wonderful." She looked down at the ground for a moment, her cheeks darkening. "Is it okay if I touch your arm again, but only for a moment?"

"Of course. But I have a better idea." He held out his hand.

Her eyes widened, and she reached for him, her small hand fitting in his palm as he wrapped his fingers around her. She braced herself, as if expecting pain, and breathed a sigh of relief when nothing happened. "Thank you."

Even though he wanted to scream at the damn injustice of it all, he smiled at her. Of course she was touch-starved.

But the longer he held her hand, the louder his alarm bells rang. The last thing he needed to do was overwhelm her. He let her hand go.

Sergei dropped her hand, and Lela took a step back from him. Had she done something wrong? But she couldn't hold his hand indefinitely, now could she?

Sergei gazed out over the foothills. "I've noticed there are few females in both the Kelmar and Lagfel villages."

Lela turned to him. "That is the case for all five clans. Over the centuries, fewer and fewer females have been born in the realm. Now the clans are in danger of dying out. Many demons here hope to find human mates so they can have children."

Sergei frowned. "How do they know they can even mate with humans?"

"Over the years, Abstatholm have gone to earth and had children with humans. That's how the realm immigration started. A half-human and half-realm-demon female petitioned the earther Demon Council to allow us to immigrate."

"I didn't know that." He cleared his throat. "I've been away from my family for a few years, and apparently I've missed a lot."

"And now you are here learning about us firsthand."

"I am, but when Aleksei introduced us, he asked me to tell you about earth as well. What would you like to know?"

"I..." Lela's mind went blank. What did she want to know? "I want to know everything."

Sergei laughed. "If that's the case, I better get talking."

And talk he did, all through their walk, and some more after they returned to see if Sabrina needed any help. Sergei stayed close, and told stories about everything he had seen in his travels throughout earth.

He said he was a photographer, but she didn't really understand what it meant. Sergei promised to send picture books to the realm to show her what the pyramids and the Great Wall of China looked like, as well as a city with millions of people. And then there were animals. She wanted to see what a bull looked like, and why Sergei would willingly let it chase him. The images in her brain were endless, but limited by the little she had to compare them to.

When it finally came time to return to the Kelmar village, Lela's head actually hurt from thinking so much.

But it was a wonderful pain to experience. Anticipation bubbled under her skin. Someday, if she was lucky, she would experience the world Sergei described.

Lela went to sleep that night and dreamed of the possibilities awaiting her on earth. And in most of those dreams, a tall male with golden-brown eyes also appeared.

CHAPTER 8

It was time to go back to earth.

Sergei studied the crowd gathered around his family to say goodbye. The past few days had been unlike anything he had ever experienced, but then he was in another world, so he shouldn't be *that* surprised.

He felt someone staring at him and turned to find Lela standing off to one side. He went over to her. "Thanks for coming to say goodbye."

"It has been nice spending time with you, Sergei."

"You too. I understand Sabrina will be staying in the realm for a while."

"Yes. She's going to travel to the other villages and help the clan members who need a healer. She's asked me to help her."

"Excellent. That makes sense, considering how well you interacted with the demons in the Lagfel village."

She beamed at him, and a tendril of warmth twisted in his gut. Time to dial it back. The last thing she needed was him complicating things for her. Lela was finally starting to gain confidence, was coming into her own. Hopefully Sabrina would be able to help her control her powers, and when that happened, there would be no stopping her.

She held out her hand, and he squeezed it gently before letting her go.

"Take care, Sergei. I hope to meet you again someday."

"You too, Lela."

Sergei went to stand with the crowd as the portal opened, but just before he stepped through, he glanced at Lela, who waved at him.

Moments later, Naya led the group through the portal, and they arrived at the Shamat community center. Kyle and Jean-Luc were waiting for them, along with a female vampire and a male who appeared human, although there was something that felt shifter about him. The blond human woman, Callie, and a set of twin boys were there as well.

When Misha came through the portal, Callie and the twins launched themselves at him. He pulled them into his arms and kissed the small female, while the boys started peppering him with question after question about the realm until Callie shushed them.

Sergei gaped at them. He had missed a lot while he was away. It looked like Misha had not only found a female, but a ready-made family as well.

Introductions were made. The female vampire was named Talia, and apparently was Jean Luc's mate. The human was Jason. Both Talia and Jason worked with Misha for the Bureau of Supernatural Relations.

Misha placed his hands on both boys' heads and walked them over to Sergei. "Matty and Luke, this is my brother, Sergei."

The boys grinned at him and held out their hands like little men. Sergei would swear Misha's chest puffed out. Sergei shook both their hands. "It's nice to meet you both."

Kyle grinned. "Thank God you're all home."

"Where's Sabrina?" Jason asked.

"Sabrina has decided to stay awhile longer to check on the health of some of the clan members, and to figure out a way to set up better medical care in the realm," Aleksei said.

Jason frowned. Was he her mate? "You left her there alone?"

"Several of my portal guards are watching over her, Jason," Naya said.

Jason's frown deepened. Definitely her mate.

"She'll be safe," Naya said, but Jason's expression remained anything but calm.

Kyle clapped her hands together. "So tell us what happened when you confronted the Kelmar. Naya only gave me bits and pieces of the story. I want the full details."

His family took turns telling the story.

"Naya was like an avenging angel," Irina said, "telling the Kelmar leader that Aleksei was not the enemy, but he still claimed blood rite."

"Then the Lagfel and Majock tried to attack Naya, and Babushka was having none of that," Misha said. "She had them hanging in the air."

"What about you?" Irina continued. "You slammed that Kelmar onto the ground as well, then Boris knocked him out."

"What!" The twins exclaimed, eyes huge, and bouncing on their toes.

Boris grinned. "I was protecting my family." He looked down at the twins, schooling his face. "You have to remember, Matty and Luke, that you should always try to solve differences without resorting to violence. Those demons attacked us, but we were hoping to avoid the Kelmar challenge."

"So if you hadn't convinced the clan leader, Aleksei would have fought the badass Kelmar demon," Kyle said.

Boris shook his head. "I would have chosen someone else from the family to fight."

"It would have been me," Irina said.

"*Mother.*"

"*Son.* I am still the most powerful, although I think Mikhail could give me a run for my money." She winked at Misha.

Sergei's stomach twisted at the banter. He had nothing to contribute to the story his family wove about their confrontation with the Kelmar.

Aleksei glanced between Boris and Irina with a smirk. "It's a good thing we don't have to worry about who would be the challenger."

"Very true," Irina said, then announced, "I don't know about the rest of you, but I need a shower, something decadent to eat, and my bed."

As the group started to disperse, Sergei froze. He wasn't sure where to go. Which was ridiculous, since this had once been his home. Misha and Callie left with the chattering boys. Boris left through the side door that led to the clan offices. Aleksei stood talking with Naya and Kyle, and the rest of the BSR team left. His grandmother was on her way toward the exit. After a moment, she hesitated and turned back to Sergei.

"Are you coming?" Irina asked.

He nodded and went with her.

"Boris has some clan work to catch up on, so you can stay with me tonight," his grandmother said.

He breathed an internal sigh of relief. His brother Misha was right the other day. Sergei had been avoiding his father. He doubted, now they were home, that he would be able to avoid him much longer.

His grandmother was very involved at the community center, so Boris had a house built for her next to the building for easy access, as well as a covered walkway they walked along now.

As soon as they entered Babushka's house, she went straight to the kitchen and opened the refrigerator, pulling out lunchmeats and cheeses.

But when she reached for a bag of hoagie rolls that had to be moldy by now, Sergei said, "We've been gone for days—"

"In the realm we've been gone for days, but here on earth we've been gone for less than a day. Time is different between the worlds." She turned on the oven.

Sergei scrubbed his hand over his face. "Could things get any stranger?"

Irina chuckled. "Not in this family, my beautiful grandson." She washed her hands at the sink. "I'm going to make ham and cheese sandwiches and pop them in the oven."

"My favorite!"

"I know. I may be over a thousand years old, but that doesn't mean my memory has left me yet." She opened the bread bag and pulled out two rolls, placing them on a baking tin. "It's good to have you home."

"I'm glad Aleksei is okay. I—"

Irina narrowed her eyes at him and her hands came to her hips. "If the next words out of your mouth, Sergei Anatoli Chesnokov, are going to be that you're leaving, I am telling you right now to rethink them."

"Grandmother, I can't stay here indefinitely."

She blew out a hard breath. "I didn't ask you to stay indefinitely. I want you to stay longer than a few minutes. You just got home. Your family needs you."

"From what I can tell, Misha has his own family now, and Aleksei is busy with running the immigration project and staring at Naya like he wants to devour her."

"You saw that too, huh?" Irina shook her head. "Don't distract me about Aleksei right now. I will make sure he doesn't screw things up with her. Let's get back to you. Your brothers still want you to be a part of their lives. And did you ever think that your father and I need you?"

Sergei's gut twisted. "Father doesn't need me."

Irina slapped heavy pieces of ham on the rolls followed by slices of Swiss cheese. "You don't know what your father needs and doesn't need, since you won't talk to him." Irina picked the pan up, slid it in the oven, and then set the timer before turning back to face him.

She gestured to the counter stool. "Take a seat. We need to have a heart-to-heart."

Sergei thought about making a break for it, but his grandmother would just use her telekinesis to pull his chicken ass back into the room. He sat down instead.

She sat down next to him and placed her hand over the fist he had clenched on the counter. "I love you, Sergei."

If she was starting out with that to soften the blow, it was about to get bad.

"But that doesn't mean I don't want to throttle you as well."

Yep, bad.

"I'll say it again. Your family *needs* you."

"It looks like everyone's doing fine without me."

Irina scowled. "Are you actually mad because people are going on with their lives *sans* Sergei? It's not like you gave any of us a choice. When you checked out, did you think we would gnash our teeth and refuse to continue living?"

Her words punched him in the gut. "Of course not."

"That's good to hear, because I didn't help raise a selfish boy."

"I couldn't stay here and live in this compound. I'm not father...or Aleksei, for that matter."

"No one expects you to be. Misha has followed a path outside the clan."

"But now it looks like he's settling down."

Irina's expression softened. "Callie and the boys are the best thing that's ever happened to your brother. He deserves to be happy, as do you and Aleksei."

Sergei looked down at his grandmother's hand, still holding tightly to his own. "I can't stay here forever."

"I'm not asking you to do that. Can you at least stay for a couple of weeks before you hit the road again? Can you promise me that?"

"Yes."

"And you also have to talk to your father. He is as stubborn as you are. Sit down and mend fences, Sergei. I said we need you, but I think you also need us. We could have lost Aleksei this week. This was our wake-up call. It's time to make amends."

The oven timer buzzed, and Irina patted his shoulder before getting up to take care of the sandwiches.

"I've got an apple pie for dessert."

Only his grandmother could read him the riot act while serving his favorite childhood foods. He owed it to her to stick around for a while and attempt to make things right.

Hell, he owed it to himself.

CHAPTER 9

Lela glanced nervously between Sabrina and her father. She wasn't sure if she was ready for whatever Sabrina had to tell her. Sabrina had come to the Kelmar village to meet with them both, and Lela was worried something awful had happened. She took a calming breath as Sabrina sat down at the small table where Lela and Saboll waited for her.

"Has something bad happened?" Lela asked.

Sabrina's eyes widened. "No. Nothing's wrong. I actually am here to give you good news, and I want to tell you personally. Lela, you have been chosen as one of the fifty who will be relocating to earth in the next immigration."

Lela slapped her hand over her mouth to hold in a sob. She never thought this would happen. She was going to earth. She turned to her father, whose eyes looked suspiciously wet.

"Father?"

His smile wobbled. "This is great news, Lela. I want you to go to earth. I'm so proud of you. You have been working alongside Sabrina for weeks now, and you've told me you would like to help other realm demons when they immigrate, and now you will be able to."

"I don't want to leave you here."

He tskd at her. "It's not like you can't visit me. One of the things Aleksei promised during the recent talks is that demons can travel back here from earth to visit their families."

She squeezed his hand as her heart sped up again at the possibilities. Then he excused himself so Lela and Sabrina could spend some time discussing next steps.

Sabrina beamed at her. "I'm so happy for you. We have a lot to do to get you ready to go to earth. The most important is teaching you how to block others from stealing your energy."

Lela's happiness ebbed. What if she couldn't do it?

Sabrina shook her finger at her. "I can see by your expression that you're worried. Don't be. We've still got a few months to get you ready."

"Don't you need to go home?"

"There's a time difference between earth and the realm. Months here equate to weeks on earth, so I can stay here for a while before I need to return home. There's still a lot to do here to get the infirmaries set up and demons trained in basic first aid."

Lela ran her fingers along the rough tabletop. "You don't have a mate waiting on earth?"

Sabrina's smile dimmed. "No. Just me."

"I'm sorry if I said something wrong."

"Not at all. There are very few Succubi left."

"Could you not mate with a human?" Lela asked before she thought better of it.

Sabrina hesitated. "I could. But I have to be careful with humans and my powers."

"But you told me you can control your powers."

"I can. It's time for you to trust me."

Lela sat up straighter. "I do trust you."

"I mean that it's time to let me touch you. If I can show you I can control my powers, it will give you hope that you can control your own."

Lela held her breath for a moment before releasing it. She could do this. She held out her arm, and Sabrina lifted her hand and hovered it above Lela's arm. Lela nodded, and Sabrina rested her fingers on her forearm. Lela tensed at the touch, but after a few seconds—nothing happened. No searing pain traveling through her body to her arm. No energy drained from her.

She burst out laughing.

Sabrina lifted her hand. "I wasn't expecting that reaction."

"I wasn't expecting it either," Lela said. "But I have hope now, like you said. We should get started."

"Okay. First, I want to understand how your energy feels to you."

"What do you mean?"

"Do you feel energy flowing through your body? Or does it sit dormant?"

"For the past few months I haven't felt anything except when the energy was pulled from me."

"What about now you've been recuperating?"

"I have felt stronger, and I guess part of that is because I can feel energy, but I've never thought about where it is in my body."

"And how does it feel when someone takes your energy?"

Lela shuddered. "Like knives traveling under my skin, slicing me open."

Sabrina scowled. "It should never feel that way. Let's do this. I want you to close your eyes and take some slow breaths. Count backwards from ten and concentrate on your breathing."

Lela did as Sabrina directed, her breaths slow and steady.

"Now search out your energy."

Lela's eyes opened, and she looked at Sabrina in question.

"You can do it. Close your eyes and let everything else fade away. Breathe and find where your strength is."

Lela closed her eyes again and thought about her breath until her mind started to flow. She sailed around inside her body, searching for that kernel of power. Finally she felt a pulse of energy in the center of her chest.

She lifted her hand and placed her fingers there. "I feel it here."

"Excellent," Sabrina said. "Can you expand the energy?"

"I don't know how."

"Imagine the energy is something you can put your hands around. You can grasp it like dough and stretch it in different directions."

Lela did as Sabrina said, wrapping imaginary hands around the heat she felt between her breasts. When she touched it, the energy skittered away from her and closed in on itself. She tried again with the same result. "It won't let me touch it."

"Okay. What if you imagine the energy to be water instead? See if you can get it to flow around your chest without touching it."

Lela concentrated on the energy, and imagined it was liquid warmth that lost its edges and started to flow through her chest. "I did it. It's moving."

"Great. See if you can get it to spread from your chest into your arms and legs and head."

Lela let the warmth spread as if she was immersed in the hot springs near her village. The energy flowed along her skin, and she took a deep breath. "I can feel it everywhere. Now what do you want me to do?"

"Relax and let it now flow to where it feels safe."

The energy shrank down again until it was a warm ball in the center of her chest. Lela slumped against the chair before opening her eyes and staring at Sabrina, who was leaning forward over the table with her hands slightly above

Lela's chest. Sabrina moved her hands away and sat back as well.

"You did a great job. I could feel your energy moving. At the end it went back to your center, in your chest, didn't it?"

"Yes. I didn't even know I contained energy like that in my body, or that I could move it."

"Now you do know, I want you to practice every day."

Lela stood. "How does moving my energy help me?"

"Because you're learning to control it. Eventually you will not only be able to move it around easily, but you should also be able to determine whether or not you want to share your energy."

Lela shook her head. "I never want to share my energy."

Sabrina narrowed her eyes at her. "I can understand why you feel that way now. But never is a long time, and it's not something you need to worry about at the moment. It's your body, and you choose when and how you want to use your energy."

The heat in her chest shrank down even further at the thought. It would be a long time, if ever, before she willingly shared her energy. She couldn't imagine any reason why she would open herself up to that again.

———◆O◆———

Callie and Misha had invited Sergei for dinner, and now he followed Irina's directions to Callie's house. When he knocked, the door opened within seconds, and he found himself looking down into the grinning face of one of the twins.

Callie came down the hall toward the entry. "Luke Nathanial Roberts, how many times have I told you not to open the door without knowing who it is?"

"But I knew who it was. You invited Sergei to dinner."

She sighed. "We'll discuss this later. Thanks for coming, Sergei."

"Thanks for inviting me. Am I early?"

She beckoned him into the entry. "No. You're right on time. You can go help Misha with the grill out back."

"I'll show you," Luke said, grabbing his hand and hauling him down the hall.

Sergei chuckled as Callie admonished Luke to slow down. Within seconds they were out on the patio. Luke let go of Sergei's hand and ran over to the biggest playset Sergei had ever seen. Matty was already climbing the ladder to go down the circular slide, and Misha was wearing an apron that said King of BBQ and keeping an eye on the grill.

Sergei laughed out loud. Misha pointed his tongs at him. "Zip it, brother. Matty and Luke got this for me today because they were so excited about us having you over for a cookout. I've got pork chops and burgers cooking. You haven't turned into a vegetarian, have you?"

"Nope. Still a carnivore."

"Can I get you a beer?"

"Not right now. Can I help with anything?"

Misha shook his head. "This should be done soon, and Callie's working on the side dishes. I'm glad you were able to come."

Sergei practically gaped at the twins as they scrambled over the playset. "That is the biggest backyard gym I have ever seen."

Misha grinned. "I saw it and knew the boys would love it."

"I'm surprised to see this domestic side of you."

"I've always wanted to find someone special, and Callie's it for me. It was an added bonus that Callie has such awesome sons."

"How did a human end up living in the compound and working for Aleksei?"

"The twins are half demon. Kelmar, to be exact." Misha glanced over at the boys across the yard before continuing. "Their father was an Abstatholm who traveled here to impregnate unsuspecting females, and was killed before the twins were born. Callie didn't know they were demon until a year ago."

"Damn."

"That's what I said when I found out. If he wasn't already dead, I would find the bastard and kill him myself. Then the Kelmar prisoner tried to kidnap the boys and take them back to the realm."

"No wonder Aleksei refused to negotiate."

"Aleksei needed help in the demon immigration office, and I asked him to give Callie a chance. She's actually a huge asset to him, and he's very fond of her and the twins."

"And what do the boys think of all this?"

Misha flipped the pork chops before responding. "They are adapting just fine. I'm warning you now that they will ask you a million questions at dinner. They want to hear about your travels and your photography, but I told them that we need some adult brother time first."

"Got it. So what do you want to discuss?"

"Nothing bad, so you can take a deep breath. Just want to hear about how you're doing."

"I'm good. The last few days have been a lot to take in."

"Not just for you. And I at least knew what was going on before I went to the realm. You were sent in unprepared."

"Your teammate Kyle was quite vocal about what I'd been missing."

Misha chuckled. "I'm sure she was."

"She's an interesting person. Doesn't hold anything back."

"You'll get used to her."

Sergei shrugged. "I don't know that I'll be running into her all that often."

"Oh, you will. Kyle is the one who petitioned the Council to let demons come to earth."

"She's the one they were talking about in the realm? She's half realm demon? I don't sense demon in her or the twins."

Misha nodded. "We think it's because they're part human and part realm. And just so you know, Kyle's a clan member. For all intents and purposes, she's your *sestra*."

"I think I'll take that beer now."

Misha's booming laugh was catching, and Sergei couldn't help grinning in response.

"How in the world did that spitfire human end up as a clan member?"

"She's actually half Majock, and she saved my life last year, so I adopted her into the clan. You should see her and Aleksei spar. It was worth it just for that alone."

The French door opened and Callie bustled out onto the patio balancing two dishes.

"Let me help," Sergei said, taking one of the bowls.

"Thanks. I'm going to grab the paper plates and a few more things," Callie said.

Sergei followed her inside and carried the condiments and pitcher of lemonade, holding the door open with his foot while Callie brought out a bowl of potato salad.

"Perfect timing," Misha said. "The meat is ready."

"Boys! It's time to eat," Callie called.

The twins ran over to the table, and Callie held up her hands. "Before you touch any food, you have to go wash up."

They looked like they were going to protest, but Misha shook his head. "You need to show Sergei where he can wash up, too."

The twins hustled into the house and called for Sergei to follow them to a bathroom. From the Superman toothbrushes and toys in the tub, it was certainly a boys' domain.

"Make sure you wash your hands good. Mom checks, and she'll send you back to do it again," one of the twins said.

Sergei stood at one sink while the other two wrestled with the soap and washed up in the other sink. When they were done, they darted back through the living room and out onto the patio. The boys held up their hands and Callie smiled.

"Looks good."

Sergei held up his hands as well. "The boys said you check."

Callie laughed. "I do. You did a good job, too."

Sergei joined everyone at the patio table, and they all dug into the food. Misha moaned at his first bite of potato salad.

"Woman, that is some of the best potato salad I have ever had."

"It's Irina's recipe."

"You make it better."

The boys' mouths dropped open, and they both said, "I'm telling!"

"You better not tell Babushka I said that."

The boys giggled, and Sergei found himself laughing as well.

"Luke, pass me the ketchup, please," Callie said.

So the twin on the left was Luke. At least now Sergei knew. "So how old are you guys?"

"Seven," Matty said.

"Are you going to school in the compound?"

"In a couple weeks, and Misha is training us about how to use our powers."

Sergei looked at Misha. "Already?"

"The boys are overachievers. They started showing powers at age six," Callie replied.

"I made a fireball at soccer practice," Matty said. "That's how we met Misha, Jean Luc, and Kyle the first time."

I just bet they did. Holy crap. *Six.* Most demons didn't start showing their powers until puberty. Except him, of course.

"I can move things with my mind," Luke piped up. "What kind of powers do you have?"

And it didn't take long for the big, ugly elephant in the room to show itself.

Misha leaned forward. "Luke, we talked about this—"

"It's okay, Misha," Sergei interrupted, then turned to the boys. "I don't have any powers, and I can't turn into my demon. I'm not special like you guys are."

The boys wore twin frowns.

"I don't understand," Luke said. "You're Misha's brother."

"Yes, but I can't make fireballs, or move things with my mind."

"But Misha said you've lived a long life," Luke said.

"I'm two hundred and forty-five years old."

"And Misha said you can feel other supernaturals?" Matty said.

"I can sense them, yes."

"And you heal faster than humans, right?" Luke asked.

"Yes." How had this turned into an inquisition?

"Then you're special," the boys announced in unison.

"And even if you couldn't do all those things, you don't have to have powers to be special. Momma's human, and she's special," Matty said.

"Yes, she is," Sergei replied, a lump aching in his throat.

Sergei glanced over at Misha and Callie, whose eyes looked suspiciously wet. Yep, the lump was growing.

"I couldn't have said that better myself," Misha said, beaming at the boys.

Thirty minutes later, Callie sent the twins and Misha to the ginormous gym set while she cleaned up. Sergei volunteered to help her.

"I'm so glad you could come over tonight. Misha was so excited."

Sergei swallowed the damn lump that kept inserting itself at the most inopportune times. "It's good to see him so happy."

"He's the best thing that's ever happened to me and the boys."

"He said the same exact thing about you earlier."

Callie handed leftovers to him, and he put them in the refrigerator. She then squirted soap into the sink and began filling it with water before looking over at him. "I'm sorry if the boys upset you earlier with their questions."

"They didn't. Out of the mouths of babes comes the real truth. They gave me a swift verbal kick to the rear. I forget that I do have things that make me demon. I'm sorry if I made you feel like you weren't special because of my earlier comments."

She shook her head. "Not at all."

"Finding out the boys were demon had to be a shock."

She washed a bowl and handed it to him to dry. "That's a bit of an understatement. I didn't know anything about the supernatural, and then my six-year-old conjured a fireball that he threw at his brother in front of his soccer team and coach. Thank God one of the parents there was a shifter, and she called the Bureau of Supernatural Relations. After that, I had the BSR on speed dial."

"The boys seem great."

"They are, but they didn't understand about their demon sides, and I had no idea what to tell them. Then Misha volunteered to help me explain things to them and to train them. I'm pretty sure he fell in love with the boys before me, but he got there eventually, and that's what matters."

"And now you live here with the boys in the compound."

"Yep. Misha is still living in his apartment, and he's letting us use his house."

Sergei frowned. "This is Misha's house? I didn't know Misha bought a house here."

"He didn't. Boris had it built for him. He's been trying to get Misha to move back here." Callie grimaced slightly. "I'm sorry."

"You have nothing to apologize for. I haven't lived here for decades. I haven't been in the States for almost a year. I don't expect Father to build me a house that will sit empty."

Well, shit. Another verbal kick to the ass, and this time it knocked him down instead of picking him up. But he wasn't going to think too much about it. He couldn't blame his father for not trying to entice him to come home. Hell, they would have to at least be able to talk to each other first.

Nope. Not thinking about it.

CHAPTER 10

Lela grinned as the energy moved through her. She practiced every day as Sabrina had recommended, and it now flowed easily where she directed it to go.

"You look happy," Sabrina said, as she joined her at the small table, sitting across from her. "You're getting a handle on your powers."

"I like being in control, but I'm not sure what I'm supposed to do next."

Sabrina placed her palms on the table. "If you can now control the movement of your energy, the next logical step is to develop the ability to decide whether you want it to leave your body...or not."

Lela's heart thumped loudly. She wouldn't be surprised if Sabrina could hear it. "In the past it has always been others taking from me."

"Because you let them."

Lela opened her mouth, and Sabrina held up her hand. "I don't mean to sound cruel. What those other demons did to you was inexcusable, and you didn't know how to harness your energy to stop them. Now we're going to work at putting the control in your hands. Are you ready to try that?"

Lela could only nod, since anxiety had a stranglehold on her throat.

"Okay. Let your energy flow around your body. While you do that, I want you to start thinking of your skin as a wall that will stop your energy from leaving. Can you do that?"

"Yes." Lela closed her eyes while energy buzzed from head to toe, bouncing against her skin. Skin that she imagined hardening into steel. "I'm doing it."

"Excellent. If you'll let me, I want to touch your arm. I won't try to take anything from you, because I'm more interested in how well you're containing your energy."

Logically, Lela knew Sabrina wouldn't take her energy without permission, but her emotions took over, and she flinched when Sabrina placed her fingers on her. Sabrina stopped, and Lela blew out a hard breath.

"I'm okay. Go ahead."

Sabrina reached slowly across the table again and placed her hand on Lela's arm. Lela continued to imagine her energy being contained behind steel walls.

After a few minutes, Sabrina lifted her hand away and smiled. "The first time you let me touch you, I could feel your energy just beneath the surface. This time your energy was muted. You're definitely getting the hang of things." Sabrina clasped her hands on the top of the table. "Would you like me to try and take some of your energy? Only a little bit. I could rest my pointer finger on your wrist."

Lela didn't answer, instead she stared at Sabrina's hands. Was she ready for that?

"We don't have to do anything today, Lela."

"No. Let's try, or else I won't know what to expect if someone tries to take from me in the future."

Once again Sabrina reached for her, her pointer finger extended. "Tell me when you want me to try drawing the energy from you." She laid her finger on her wrist, and this time Lela didn't jump.

Lela looked up into Sabrina's face and waited. Her energy bounced sporadically under her skin, and she forced herself to concentrate on building the wall. After several drawn-out seconds, she nodded. A slight pull on her wrist, and her energy moved down her arm as if it had a mind of its own.

Panic started to set in until Sabrina spoke softly to her. "Block me. Harden your skin, keep what is yours."

Lela stared at her own wrist. Walls hardened, and the pull disappeared.

After a few more seconds Sabrina lifted her hand. "You did it! You blocked me."

Lela giggled, stifling the urge to jump up and down. "I did, didn't I?"

Sabrina chuckled. "Yep. We'll keep practicing this as well. As you get stronger, I'll increase the strength of my attempt to pull the energy, but I'm sure you'll have no trouble blocking me."

Lela had never felt this much in control in her entire life. It was a wondrous feeling. If she could learn to block whoever tried to steal from her, she'd be able to have a normal life. Something she had never dared to hope for in the past. She wanted to shout her news to everyone in the realm. Sergei popped into her mind. She wished he were here so she could show him. Would she ever see him again?

Now she was part of the immigration, would she be lucky enough to live near him? She pushed down those hopeful wishes. Sergei told her about his travels, and she had a hard time grasping the size of earth, but she highly doubted he would be anywhere near her new home, and even if he was, he wouldn't stay for long.

Sergei walked through the Shamat compound streets, taking in all the changes. Even in the two years since he last visited, the community had grown, with more houses and more families.

When he reached the street with Callie and the boys' house, he found his brother sitting on the front porch, looking way too comfortable in a ridiculously large rocking chair. "Out for a stroll, brother? It's a good night for it. I love warm summer evenings."

Sergei joined him on the porch. "Taking in the changes. You have a nice house."

Misha stared at him for an awkward moment. "Callie and the boys live here. I'm still in my apartment."

"Where are Callie and the boys?"

"The boys are in bed. Callie and Kyle went out for dinner and drinks. They both could use a break with how busy work has been for Callie, so I volunteered for babysitting duty."

"She probably needs a break from Aleksei. Do you have any idea what's wrong with him? He's even more of a bossy ass than usual."

Misha frowned. "He's actually changed for the better over the past few months. But something happened. Naya left a few days ago, and he's been biting everyone's head off ever since."

"I thought there was something going on between those two. I might be clueless about some things, but the looks those two were giving each other were combustible."

"Yep. We can ask Kyle and Callie when they get back if they have any insights."

"Maybe it would be best if I left," Sergei said.

"Why?"

"I got the distinct impression that Kyle doesn't like me."

"She doesn't *know* you. It takes a lot for Kyle to accept someone. You have to earn her trust."

"Why do I get the feeling that's not easy to accomplish?"

"Because it isn't. But once she pulls you into her circle, she'll protect you like a lioness with her cub. I told you she and Aleksei butt heads all the time, but she respects the hell out of him. She was all ready to storm the realm to save Aleksei, but she stayed behind to run things here."

A red car came down the street and slowed before turning into the driveway. Callie and Kyle climbed out of the car and came up onto the porch. Callie gave Misha a quick kiss before she and Kyle sat on the porch swing.

"Did the boys fight you about going to bed?" Callie asked.

"Nope. They were angels."

Callie's eyebrows rose. "Angels? I smell something rotten. When was the last time you checked on them?"

"Not too long ago. They were both asleep."

Callie hopped up. "I'm going to make sure they're still that way. I'll be right back."

Kyle sighed happily as she pushed the porch swing back and forth.

"We were just talking about you, little one."

Kyle looked from Misha to Sergei. "All good things, I'm sure."

"Absolutely. Have you noticed how cranky Aleksei has been lately?"

"Aleksei was born cranky, but he has dialed it up to a ten lately. I think he misses Naya."

"Do you know what happened between them?" Misha asked.

Kyle shrugged. "She took off suddenly. When I try to find out what's going on through our telepathic link, she won't tell me why she left. Just gives me a song and dance about needing to be in the realm to work on relationships there."

"You don't believe her?" Sergei asked.

"It's a bunch of bull-pucky. She can babble about forming relationships in the realm, but I think the truth is she's avoiding them here."

"Aleksei won't talk to me, either," Misha said. "I tried to question him the other day, and I swear smoke was rising from his fingertips."

"So whose head won't he bite off?" Kyle asked.

"Don't look at me," Sergei said. "He bites my head off during normal conversations."

"How about Babushka?" Misha answered.

"A possibility," Sergei said. "He won't yell at her, but he'll dig his damn heels in and not talk to her."

Kyle nodded. "I agree. What about Callie?"

"What about me?" Callie said as she joined them again.

"We're discussing Aleksei's crappy mood. We think you're a great person to watch out for him and see if you can get at the truth about what's bothering him."

"Absolutely. I'm very worried about him."

Kyle rubbed her hands together. "Okay, then. Let's get Callie her magnifying glass and secret decoder ring, and she can start spying for us."

Misha chuckled. "I think you've been hanging around with the twins too much."

"It's not much different from putting up with your and Aleksei's antics."

"You should have seen Aleksei and Sergei as children. Sergei was Aleksei's shadow. He tried to do everything Aleksei did, even though he was five years younger."

Misha's words were bittersweet. Sergei wasn't that child anymore, but he'd been missing out on a lot with his family.

"The boys were asleep, yes?" Misha asked.

Callie chuckled. "If by sleep, you mean they had flashlights and were reading comic books under the blankets, then yes."

Kyle burst out laughing as she stood and walked down the porch steps. "Wow, I've got to get going, but not before I tell you your babysitting skills aren't the best, Mish."

Callie's smile grew. "He just needs more practice."

Misha's eyes widened at Sergei. "Stick up for me, brother."

Sergei held up his hands. "Nope. I'm not going up against these two. I know how it would turn out."

Kyle stared at him for a moment before nodding. "Smart answer. The jury's still out, but there might be hope for you yet."

Wasn't that the story of his life? "Thanks—I think."

After Kyle left, Misha moved over to the swing and sat down next to Callie. "You might have made some progress with Kyle, Sergei."

"That was progress?"

"The first time she met Aleksei, she called him to task in front of a group of people. Told him he was rude and condescending. A couple weeks ago she told him to quote pull the stick out of his ass end quote. Those are memories I'll cherish forever," Misha said.

Sergei laughed. "I wish I would have seen it."

And to his surprise, he really did.

Callie started to get up and Misha placed his hand on her leg. "Where are you going?"

"To make sure the boys are asleep."

"I'll do it. Like you said, I need the practice."

Misha went into the house.

"Did you have a good time with Kyle tonight? Misha said you needed to blow off some steam since work is busy for you."

"It's been especially hard since we're gearing up for a much bigger immigration this time. Fifty demons. And on top of that, I have to pull together supplies that need to be taken to the realm, and I haven't lined anyone up to do that yet."

"I can do it," Sergei said.

"Really?" Callie perked up. "Are you sure?"

"Yes. I'd be happy to help. If I'm going to stick around for a while, I want to be useful. But I have one condition. I don't want Aleksei to know."

Callie's puzzled look prompted him to explain.

"I don't want Aleksei to try to manage this. He has enough on his plate."

"Fine. We have a deal."

Sergei nodded. He might not be that little kid who followed his big brother around anymore, but that didn't mean he couldn't help him out.

CHAPTER 11

Lela stood to the side and watched Sabrina examine the ailing elder. She was a good healer, willing to listen, and patient with the clan members who were leery of her. Today's visitor was a Palthat demon who complained of weakness in his limbs when standing and walking. As he pointed down, Lela followed his gesture and stared at his legs, but after a moment, she blinked. What was she seeing?

It was as if his skin had become see-through, and she could see his energy flowing through his veins and tissues. Although flowing was not the right word, it barely trickled down through his legs, as if something blocked it. On the other hand, his torso and arms looked good. Energy moved quickly through the top of his body...until it pooled at the base of his spine.

Sabrina ran her hands along the clan member's legs.

"Check his back, Sabrina," Lela said.

Sabrina stood and ran her hands along his spine until she rested them above the spot where his energy pooled. "There's something going on here. It could be a pinched nerve or disc. I want to schedule some time for you to return and let me massage that area. In the meantime, I'm going to give you some medicine to help with any inflammation."

After the elder left, Sabrina turned to Lela with a puzzled look. "Are you going to tell me how you knew I needed to check his back?"

Lela glanced away from her. "The same way you did. I could see his energy was blocked."

"Yes it was, but I have to touch or rest my hands just above someone to know that. You were standing across the room."

"It was as if I could see inside him. I don't know how to explain it exactly."

"Interesting," Sabrina said. "Are you ready to see the next person?"

Before Lela could respond, they heard excited voices outside the hut. Had something happened? They hurried outside to see a group of clan members surrounding someone. Someone in human form, from the look of his blond hair. After a moment he turned and looked at them. It was Sergei! Why was he here?

He was standing next to a large cart on wheels with heaps of clothes and other items. The Palthat leader joined Sergei and grasped his hand. "Welcome."

"I've brought some supplies for your village, per the agreement you worked out with Aleksei."

"Excellent. Would you like to stay for our midday meal? You must be hungry from traveling to the other villages."

"Thank you. A meal would be good before I go see the Dragans."

Lela stood back. She was getting more confident in her ability to control her power, but she wasn't ready to test it in a crowd. As if Sergei could feel her gaze on him, he turned and saw her, then sidestepped the clan members looking at the supplies and walked over to her.

"I was hoping to see you on this trip." He smiled. "I have something for you."

Her heart sped up. What could he have brought her?

Sabrina made her way over to them.

"Sabrina. How are things going?" Sergei asked.

"Good. We're setting up a medical hut with supplies in each clan village, and I've been traveling to the five clans for office hours. I have also been training those in the clans who have an aptitude for healing." She gestured toward Lela. "Lela is helping me set everything up."

"I'm not surprised."

Sabrina looked between the two of them. "Lela, why don't you take a break and have lunch with Sergei?"

"What about you?"

"I'm going to grab something to eat and take it into the hut so I can relax for a few minutes."

Lela led him to the village center, where several pots of food cooked over an open flame. Lela stifled a laugh as the clan members loaded Sergei's dish with food. They sat down away from the crowd.

Lela gestured to his almost-overflowing bowl. "It appears the clan members are very happy you visited them today."

"If I eat all this, I won't be able to walk to the next village."

They ate in silence for a few minutes until Lela couldn't contain her curiosity any more. "What did you bring me?"

Sergei laughed. "Impatient, aren't we?"

Lela's face heated under his gaze. "Yes."

He pulled off a bag he had strapped to his back. "When I was here before, I promised I would send you books with pictures of earth."

He pulled out several books and placed them in her lap. Her hands shook as she ran her hand over the cover of the top book.

"Go ahead and open it."

She flipped open the cover and touched shiny paper covered with bursts of color. They weren't drawings or words. Instead these...pictures, as Sergei called them...held magic. They captured a world shrunk down into little squares. She looked up at him.

"This is magical."

He chuckled. "You haven't even turned the first page yet."

She blinked. "Thank you." She flipped the page and gasped. And as each page turned, earth unfolded before her. *This* would be her new home.

Sergei chuckled. "I love seeing you like this. It's like experiencing things again through new eyes."

"You have been to these places?" She asked, looking up at him.

"Many of them, yes."

"Then you must tell me about them while I look at the pictures."

Sergei's eyebrows rose. "Okay." And as she moved from picture to picture, Sergei told her stories that weaved together a vision of her new world.

A shadow fell over the book, and she looked up to find a Palthat demon towering over them.

"You're the female everyone's been talking about," he said, his eyes raking over her.

Lela inched closer to Sergei. "I don't know what you mean."

"You can share your energy. I think you should share with me."

Sergei set the book to the side and stood. "Sharing means voluntarily giving it. Not stealing."

The demon scowled. "Stay out of this, earther."

Lela scrambled to her feet. "Stop!"

Sergei stepped in front, as if to shield her. "Walk away, now."

The demon chuckled, but it was a rough, almost menacing sound. "I don't think you can stop me, even if you want to." A fireball began to form in his palm.

Lela would not let Sergei get hurt for her. She started to step around him, but he held up his arm to stop her. "Don't, Lela. Get out of here."

The demon glanced past them and the cocky grin left his face.

Lela looked behind her to find the portal guard and Sabrina standing a couple of steps away. And while the guard was intimidating enough, Sabrina was terrifying. Not that she looked any different, but power was emanating from her like a blast of heat.

The demon closed his hand, snuffing out the fireball.

The Palthat leader strode over to the growing group with two large demons following behind him. "Enough, Sarun!" He gestured to the two behind him. "Go with them. I will deal with you in a moment."

The demon stalked away, flanked by the two guards.

The Palthat leader turned to Lela. "Did he hurt you?"

"No. He didn't get near me." *Because Sergei shielded her.*

"I'm sorry. Nothing like this will happen again. I will make sure of it." He looked at Lela, and then Sergei and Sabrina in turn. "I want you to feel safe in our village. Please accept my apology."

After a few more reassurances from the leader, the crowd dispersed, leaving Sergei and Lela alone.

"Are you okay?" Sergei asked.

"Yes. I was more worried about you."

Sergei's eyes tightened on her, and she realized he had taken her statement the wrong way.

"Not because you are powerless, but because a fireball is not something to mess with." Lela rested her hand on his arm. "Thank you for protecting me."

Sergei's eyes widened at her gesture. "You touched me."

"Yes. I know you can't hurt me, but I have also been working with Sabrina to learn how to control my powers. I have to be ready for demons like Sarun, and for the immigration."

"Did you say prepare you for immigration?"

"Yes. I am coming to earth in the next group. I'll be there in a few months."

His frown changed into a grin. "That's great! But the next group will be there in a few weeks, not months."

"Sabrina has explained that time moves differently in the worlds."

Sergei nodded. "Right. I knew that. I'm so happy for you."

"Will you be traveling back to the realm?" Lela asked.

"I don't know for sure. I'll have to see if they need help with the next set of supplies."

They returned to the cart, where Sabrina met them and handed Sergei a piece of paper. "This is a list of medical supplies I need here. Will you see what you can do to get them?"

"Sure. I'll talk to Callie."

Lela watched Sergei and the portal guard leave the village. After a few moments, she turned to find Sabrina staring at her.

"What?"

"Sergei is an interesting male."

"Yes. He has been very kind to me."

"And protective."

"He was willing to face off with that demon even though he is powerless." Lela paused before continuing. "However, I just discovered that you definitely are not powerless."

Sabrina shrugged. "I'm normally a lover not a fighter, but that doesn't mean I don't have moments. I find the threat of power deters most confrontations. Enough about me. We were talking about Sergei. When you get to earth, you might be able to spend more time with him."

"I would like that, but Sergei is a traveler. He moves around the world."

"Maybe he moves around the world because he hasn't found something or someone yet to keep him in one spot."

Before Lela could respond, a clan member approached Sabrina, and she led them into the hut.

Lela pondered Sabrina's insight. Sergei wasn't going to stop exploring to spend time with her on earth. She couldn't expect him to do that. Hope, maybe—expect, no.

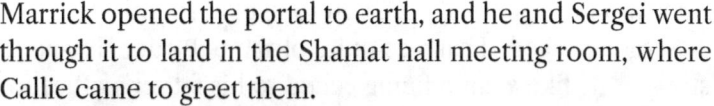

Marrick opened the portal to earth, and he and Sergei went through it to land in the Shamat hall meeting room, where Callie came to greet them.

Marrick couldn't be persuaded to stay for long, claiming that he was needed back in the realm.

Once the portal shut behind him, Callie asked, "How did things go?"

Sergei had decided before he arrived back on earth not to bring up the almost-confrontation with the demon. If Aleksei found out, he probably wouldn't allow him to help anymore, and he wasn't about to be relegated to the sidelines because he lacked demon powers.

Sergei pulled Serena's list out of his pocket. "Everything is good. The clans were very appreciative of the supplies, Sabrina gave me a list of medical supplies she needs, and I'm going to make a list of things I think would be useful as well. The realm reminds me of many of the remote villages here on earth that I've visited over the years. There are definitely things we can supply that would be helpful."

"Thank you. Aleksei asked the clans what they wanted, but they can't ask for things they don't know exist, right?"

When Callie and Sergei walked into the hallway, the door leading to the clan offices opened and Boris stepped into the corridor. Had he been standing on the other side of the door waiting for him?

"Sergei. I was looking for you earlier. Do you have some spare time? I think it would be good to catch up."

"Sure."

"Wonderful. Would you like to come to my house for dinner?"

Panic set in. "I..."

Boris' eyes tightened on him. "I invited Mother as well. I thought she would be a buffer, since you don't seem to want to be alone with me. I'll see you tonight at six thirty."

Sergei cringed. That was quite blunt, but true. He had to stop acting like a child being called to his father's office for punishment.

Callie cleared her throat, and he jumped slightly. He'd forgotten she was standing there.

"I don't know what your history is with your father, but I think you should give him a chance. He truly is a softy under all his bluster. The boys actually got him to play frisbee with them the other day. I told him to not wear a suit when he comes over next time. Less wear and tear on the Armani."

Sergei laughed. "Thanks for the visual, I needed that."

A few hours later, Sergei arrived at his father's house, and stood outside the door trying to center himself...if he believed in that sort of thing. He had planned to walk there with Irina since he was staying with her, but she left early, declaring she had to oversee the meal. Which meant she would probably cook it herself.

He took another breath and knocked on the door. Boris opened it and smiled at him. He had changed out of his ever-present suit and put on a pair of casual pants and shirt. Sergei's jeans probably didn't pass muster, but it was too late now.

"Come in," he said. "Your grandmother is in the kitchen, taking over, as usual."

Sergei followed him down the hall, but instead of going toward the kitchen, Boris took him into the dining room, where he went over to the sideboard, which held a small bar.

"Something to drink?"

"Whatever you're having."

Sergei expected to see him reach for the top shelf vodka Boris kept, but he uncapped a bottle of whiskey. One of Sergei's favorites.

"When did you start drinking whiskey?" Sergei asked as Boris handed him the glass.

"You raved about it when you returned from one of your trips to Scotland, and I decided to try it."

Sergei took a fortifying sip before glancing around the room, pausing at the painting above the fireplace. The family portrait Boris had commissioned when Sergei and Aleksei were still children. Misha was already an adult, but he had also posed for the painting. And, sitting in a highbacked chair with "her men," as she liked to call them, surrounding her, was his mother.

She had been a gorgeous woman, with long, dark hair and honey-brown eyes. Seeing the pleased smile on her face still tore Sergei's heart out.

"You have your mother's eyes," Boris said behind him.

Sergei spun away from the picture. "I'm sorry."

Boris frowned. "Why in the world would you be sorry for that?"

Because his father only had to look at him to be reminded of what he had lost. And because Sergei was the reason he had lost her.

Thankfully, his grandmother joined them just then and stopped him from blurting out the truth.

"Food will be ready in a few minutes. Boris actually did a good job with it."

Boris grinned. "Thank you, Mother. I have been cooking for myself for a while now, you know."

Irina waved her hand. "Are you planning to offer me a drink?"

His father bowed slightly. "Apologies for my bad manners. What would you like to drink?"

"Sex on the Beach."

"I don't have the ingredients for that, and you know it."

"What about a Screaming Org—"

"Do not finish that sentence!" Boris blurted, actually squeaking at the end. "Is it impossible for you to behave?"

Irina laughed. "Behaving is boring, son."

Boris glared at her.

"Fine, I'll have Moskovskaya, neat."

Boris handed her the glass of vodka, and she took a sip before glancing between the two of them. "What did I miss while I was in the kitchen? Did you make up with him, Boris?"

Sergei's stomach bottomed out. He had thought having his grandmother here would be a good thing. On second thought, he should have known better.

"Sergei just got here," Boris answered noncommittally, like the politician he was.

"Father doesn't need to make up with me. I am the disappointment."

Boris jolted back as if someone punched him, letting out a curse in Russian. "Why would you think you're a disappointment to me? I am proud of you, Sergei. How could you think otherwise?"

Sergei set the glass down for fear he would shatter it in his tight grip. "Do you really need a list? I am not like Misha and Aleksei. I can't live up to them and your expectations."

Irina slammed her glass down on the table. "Sergei Anatoli Chesnokov! You need to come with me, this instant."

"Mother—"

"No Boris, I am done sitting back and watching this painful dance the two of you are doing."

Irina stomped out of the dining room and threw open the door across the hall, gesturing for Sergei to enter the room. It was his father's study, lined with bookshelves with the various books and knickknacks Boris had collected over the centuries.

"Look behind you," Irina demanded.

Sergei turned and gaped at the wall behind his father's desk. There were a half dozen photos on the wall. *His* photos. One from a village in the Sudan, another of the Swiss Alps, yet another of the bustling streets of Tokyo.

Sergei swallowed. Hard. He turned to look at his father, who stood in the doorway.

"I am proud of you, son. You have accomplished a lot, and you're very gifted. No one in the family has your talent. You remind me of your mother in that way. She was the artist in the family."

Sergei jerked his head side to side. "No. Don't compare me to Mother. I don't deserve that."

"Why would you say that?" he asked.

"Because I killed her!"

Boris blanched. "You didn't kill her. Her heart gave out."

"I heard the doctor the night he told you she wouldn't make it. He said her heart had weakened after she had me. That she shouldn't have risked another pregnancy."

Irina gasped and covered her mouth.

Boris opened his arms to Sergei. "Your mother loved you. *I* love you. She lived for ten years after you were born. When she found out she was pregnant with you, she wept tears of joy."

"I don't have powers. I'm defective, and she died—"

"Enough!" Boris roared. "Do you think your mother gave birth to you for powers? You are insulting her memory. She loved you. Before she died, she made me promise to make you see your worth. And *I* failed her. When she died, I lost my way, and your grandmother had to step in.

"I should have put aside my grief and taken care of you, but I failed you as a father. If anyone should be ashamed, it should be me. I should be begging for *your* forgiveness."

Sergei looked away from his father's red face into Irina's tear-stained one. He closed his eyes for a moment before facing his father again to see a tear roll down Boris's cheek.

Boris stepped closer and clasped his hands on Sergei's shoulders. "You have carried this pain around for centuries, Sergei. I am so sorry. If I could go back in time and take it from you, I would. And in case you are still unsure. I have never been disappointed in you. I have been saddened that you separated from the family, but I am and always will be proud of you."

When Boris pulled Sergei into his arms and hugged him. Sergei's eyes filled, and he let the tears fall. Tears he'd kept inside for hundreds of years. His father was proud of him.

Now he had to learn to be proud of himself.

CHAPTER 12

Lela and Sabrina had just finished with the last Kelmar patient of the day when a portal guard burst into the hut. "We need your help."

"What happened?" Sabrina asked.

"Marrick sent me to get you. Something is wrong with Naya. She's unconscious."

"Where is she?"

"Her hut in the in-between. I'll take you to her."

Sabrina grabbed one of her doctor bags while Lela grabbed the other. "I'm coming with you."

It took an hour to travel from the realm to the in-between. Once they moved through the portal, they jogged through the field toward the small huddle of huts.

While they jogged, Lela studied the area. She had never been in the in-between before, and was actually surprised the guard had not protested her coming there. Now, as she ran through the field with Sabrina, she realized it wasn't all that different than the realm.

Lela followed Sabrina into the hut the portal guard pointed out, where they found Marrick standing by the bed with his arms crossed, and Naya lying on the bed with her own arms crossed. Clearly they were having a battle of wills.

"Naya, will you tell me what happened?" Sabrina asked as she set down her bag. Lela placed the other bag on the end of the bed and backed up to the door to stay out of the way.

"I'm fine. Marrick overreacted."

"You passed out."

From across the room, Lela narrowed her eyes and concentrated. Naya's energy bubbled throughout her body. Unlike many of the ailing patients Sabrina saw, there was nothing blocking Naya's energy flow. In contrast, she actually had a considerable amount of energy, especially in her abdomen.

Wait. Lela stared at her abdomen. It was as if her energy was fighting against itself. No, more like two different energy flows trying to occupy the same space. Lela bit back a gasp and backed out the door to give the three of them some privacy.

Some time later, Sabrina emerged from the hut and sat down with Lela on the stumps used for outside seating.

"I was surprised to find you missing when I turned around."

"I wanted to give you time to explain things to her about the baby."

Sabrina's eyes widened. "I should have realized you would sense it."

"Yes. I didn't think it was appropriate for me to interrupt their time with you, especially after I realized that Marrick isn't the father."

Sabrina snapped her head in her direction. "How do you know that?"

"The baby's energy is somewhat like Naya's, but it varies. It doesn't match Marrick's energy at all."

"You are amazing. Your powers are growing."

"Even if I hadn't sensed that, I saw how Naya stood up for Aleksei with my father. She loves him."

"Yeah. I think you're right."

"Is she going to go to earth to have the baby?"

Sabrina shook her head. "She plans to stay here. Naya doesn't want anyone to know right now that she's pregnant, especially Aleksei."

Lela frowned. "Aleksei has a right to know about his child. And it's not something she will be able to hide for long."

Sabrina sighed. "She's in shock right now. For some reason she didn't know she was in her cycle when she was with Aleksei, so she had no idea she was pregnant. Once she absorbs it, she'll tell Aleksei. I don't see those two staying away from each other for long. But I can't interfere with that. On earth, I have to adhere to an oath as a doctor. I'm not allowed to reveal a patient's health condition to anyone unless the patient gives me permission."

"You're talking to me about it right now."

"I didn't tell you she was pregnant. You figured that out yourself."

"Earth rules are complicated."

"Yes, they are. Mainly because earth is complicated. Here in the realm, things are simpler and more straightforward. On earth there are humans and other supernaturals to throw a wrench into things.

"What is a wrench?"

Sabrina chuckled. "I don't know how to explain it, exactly. It's a saying. A wrench is a kind of tool, but the saying means that you think something is going to work one way, and something or someone comes along and changes it completely."

"Like when the earthers announced we would be allowed to leave the realm after a millennium of captivity."

"Exactly. I'm going to check on Naya once more before we head back."

Sabrina disappeared into the hut as Lela tried to sort through everything Sabrina told her. Up to this moment, the idea of going to earth excited her. Now her excitement was offset by trepidation. Would she ever learn enough about the world where she would soon live? And even if she did, would she understand how to fit in?

———◄O►———

Sergei's phone rang, jarring him awake. He looked at the clock on the bedside stand as he reached for his phone—six am.

"What's wrong, Misha?"

"We need to knock some sense into our brother. Callie is worried sick about him. When she comes into the office in the morning, he's already there, and he stays after she leaves. She's found clothes in his office. She doesn't think he's going home anymore, just working nonstop."

"What's the plan?"

"You and I are going to stage an intervention on Aleksei."

"An intervention? Seriously?"

"That's what this family does now. You missed the one they staged on me."

His family was over the top. "When are we going to have this intervention?"

"Meet me at the compound gym in fifteen minutes. Aleksei should be there now."

Twelve minutes later, Sergei walked up to the gym door where Misha stood watching. Sergei stopped next to him. "What's going on?"

"I just caught the last few minutes of Aleksei running until he almost fell off the machine. Now look at him."

Aleksei stood on the right side of the gym where a long, fireproof hall had been fashioned for target practice. Fireball after fireball flew from Aleksei's fingertips until the far wall smoked from the assault.

"Aleksei!" Misha hollered.

Aleksei jerked, and the fireball he threw landed off-target. He spun around and glared at them both.

"What the hell are you doing?" Misha asked.

"What does it look like?" Aleksei snapped.

"It looks like you're ready to fall over," Sergei responded.

"You've been working nonstop for weeks, and now we find you working out like a demon possessed." Misha glared at Aleksei. "And you look like you've lost weight. If you keep up this pace, you're going to make yourself sick."

"I have a lot to do."

"Then ask for help," Sergei said.

Aleksei glared at Sergei. "Pretty ironic, coming from you. Why would I ask you for help when you'll be hitting the road any day now? That's what you do, Sergei. You run."

Misha frowned. "Aleksei—"

Sergei held up his hand. "Don't play peacekeeper, Misha. Just because I haven't stayed here doesn't mean I ran away. It's not like I can be much help anyway."

Aleksei barked out a harsh laugh. "What a load of bullshit. Why can't you help? Because you don't have any powers? I've got news for you. The only person who cares about that is you. Does it mean you think humans are worthless because they're powerless too? Do you think Misha loves Callie any less because she's human and apparently weak in your eyes?"

Sergei locked his legs so he didn't get into his brother's face. "Of course not. You're just saying this now because the truth is out, and everyone knows Misha is more powerful than the almighty Aleksei. It's a hard fall from your pedestal, isn't it? Especially now you won't be clan leader."

"Sergei, don't!" Misha growled. "You don't know what's going on."

Aleksei grimaced and shook his head. "Of course not, because he's never here. And that's what you don't understand. Family is there for each other—"

"—I came home when you were in trouble."

"You didn't let me finish. Family is there for both the bad and the good, the big and the small."

"I can't stay here all the time."

"You don't have to be here physically to stay connected to us," Misha said.

Sergei's mouth dropped open. "Shit. I can't believe you're on his side."

"I'm not on anyone's side," Misha barked. "I want us to be in each other's lives."

"Because it's such a barrel of fun?"

"Because I miss you. Because I think we're stronger together than apart. And instead of you two tearing into each other, maybe I should kick both your asses and give you a time out before we continue this conversation!"

Sergei gawked at Misha, and from Aleksei's expression, he was just as surprised at the outburst. Of the three of them, Misha was the slowest to anger.

Misha crossed his arms. "Now I have your attention, perhaps we should start this discussion over again. Tell us what's wrong, Aleksei. Does it have to do with a certain portal guard who no longer visits earth?"

Aleksei shoved past them toward the door. "I need to get cleaned up and ready for work."

"Now who's running?" Sergei called after him.

Aleksei spun around and faced them. "What do you want me to say? That Naya twists my insides into knots, and I think about her every damn minute of every damn day? She doesn't want to be with me. She doesn't want to be tied down. She wants to be free after the immigration."

Aleksei looked away. And the three of them stood in silence.

After a moment, Misha spoke in a softer voice. "That doesn't sound like Naya. She is as honorable as you are."

Aleksei grimaced. "It doesn't matter. She claims she is going to travel the world with Marrick. And when I confronted him, he told me he's in love with her."

"And?" Misha asked.

Aleksei threw his hands up. "Isn't it enough?"

Misha and Sergei exchanged a look before Misha continued. "Do you know if she's in love with him? Because that's the only answer that matters."

After a few minutes, Misha escorted Aleksei off to the showers and also planned to make him eat something before he went to the office. Misha was right, Aleksei was losing weight, and that scared Sergei. His older brother was normally unflappable. Now? He was vulnerable.

And Sergei had just taunted him. Nasty words about Misha being the most powerful. *Damn.* How was he ever going to repair things between him and Aleksei? His father was right. After his mother died, Irina stepped in and helped raise him, but Aleksei did the same. Aleksei was fifteen when their mother died, and he took his ten-year-old brother under his wing.

Now was the time for Sergei to help him any way he could. He hurried to the immigration offices, hoping he would beat Aleksei there. He was in luck. Callie sat alone in the office.

"Callie, we need to talk."

"Is Aleksei okay?" she asked.

"He will be." If he and Misha had any say in the matter. "I want to do more to help with the immigration, before Aleksei works himself to death."

She frowned. "I know. I don't even know if he's sleeping."

"I don't know how to help him. Misha told him to fight for Naya, but he's not there yet. In the meantime, the only way to help his stubborn ass is to take some of the burden off him."

"That's so wonderful of you."

Sergei sat down next to her desk. "Remember what we discussed last time. I don't want him to know I'm helping, because he'd fight me on it. Give me something to do that he isn't micromanaging right now."

Callie pursed her lips for a moment before responding. "There isn't much he isn't overseeing right now. I have another delivery of items to the realm like before. Could you help with that? With everything going on right now with the immigration, I can't devote the time to it."

"I can make another run, sure. But I think I can take the planning on as well."

Callie practically bounced in her seat. "Excellent! Do you want to discuss the details now, before he gets here?"

"Yeah. Misha is forcing him to eat breakfast this morning, so we have a few minutes."

"Then we better get to work."

CHAPTER 13

Lela closed her eyes as she took deep breaths, listening to Sabrina's voice. Today, for the first time, Sabrina was teaching her how to change from demon to her human form.

"Relax, Lela. Let your energy transform you. Find the other half you have buried inside you, and bring it out of hiding."

Warmth bubbled under Lela's skin, and she opened her eyes to look at her hands as her orange skin lightened to pale cream, starting with her fingertips and running up her arm.

"You did it!" Sabrina said, with sparkling eyes and a grin, as she held up a mirror for Lela.

"I did," Lela whispered as she looked at human self. Her eyes had turned a green color, and her hair had changed from its normal bright red to a muted tone.

"You will be well ahead of the other immigrants when you get to earth."

"Should I be?"

"What do you mean?"

"I was thinking that it would help all the immigrants to learn more about earth ahead of time. And why couldn't we teach them to change into their human form as well?"

Sabrina gaped at her.

"Did I say something wrong?" Lela asked.

"No. You said something perfect. I'm sorry I didn't think to help with this earlier."

"We still have another two months before we immigrate to earth. Can you stay longer to help?"

Sabrina nodded. "Two months equates to about two weeks in earth time. I can definitely stick around and help. I also think we should have Naya reach out to Kyle and get some more picture books about earth. That way, when we do our rounds in the villages, we can also teach those scheduled for the immigration, and anyone who wants to listen, about earth."

"And we can help them with their human side?"

"Absolutely. I think it would also make sense for me to do the preliminary exam I normally conduct on their arrival day now instead of waiting."

Lela's heart fluttered at the words of praise. "Wouldn't it be great to arrive on earth in our human forms?"

Sabrina laughed. "I agree! Let's not tell anyone, so we don't spoil the surprise. We'll just ask for the books and leave it at that."

Lela giggled. When was the last time she had felt excited and eager about what was to come? This was definitely something she could get used to.

A few days later, Sabrina arrived at the Kelmar village, where Lela sat outside her hut.

"Naya heard from Kyle. The medicines I requested, plus clothing, tools, and the books should be arriving shortly. Will you help me with distribution?"

"Of course."

"Excellent. The plan is for Marrick to open the portal to earth and bring back the supplies. We'll set up a distribution site at the edge of the forest, which is a centralized location for all five clans. That way the clans can send members to pick up the supplies and take them to their villages."

"That will save time." Lela gestured to the village square. "Are you ready to train the immigrants in how to bring out their human side?"

Sabrina followed her gaze to the crowd. "There are only ten Kelmars immigrating this time."

Lela shrugged. "The immigrants aren't the only ones who are interested in learning. Many want to learn in preparation for when it's their turn. I have also been showing the clan the books Sergei brought me. Once we get more books, we can distribute them in the other four villages."

They walked to the square, where most of Lela's clan circled them.

Sabrina took in the crowd. "Do you want to all learn to change to your human form?"

Several shouted affirmations and head-nods later, Sabrina raised her hands. "All right, everyone! It's perfectly fine if you all want to be a part of this. It won't hurt to learn how to change now, even if you aren't yet scheduled for the immigration."

"Why don't you show them how to do it, Lela?"

Lela nodded, although her nerves jangled. She hadn't used her powers in front of her clan before. She closed her eyes while Sabrina spoke to her, putting her at ease and hopefully the other clan members as well.

Lela listened to Sabrina's calm voice walking her through the process, and let those around her melt away as she concentrated on her energy. A few moments later a ripple of gasps sounded around her. She opened her eyes and glanced at her skin. She had transformed into her human form.

A hand reached out and touched her arm. Seconds later, the elder jerked his hand back. "I'm sorry, Lela. I shouldn't have touched you."

"It's okay. Nothing happened."

"Who's ready to learn how to change?" Sabrina asked the crowd.

The chorus of "me" and "yesses" was even louder and more boisterous this time.

Sabrina rolled up her sleeves. "Okay, everyone sit down and close your eyes, and I'll lead you through the relaxation technique Lela just used. Remember, it might take several tries before you're able to turn, so don't get discouraged."

Lela smiled down at her clan members as they sat and listened to Sabrina like attentive children. Now everyone was sitting, Lela could see the entire square. On the outskirts stood Marrick and Sergei.

Had they seen her change to human? While Marrick watched Sabrina and the crowd, Sergei gazed directly at her and smiled.

Her face warmed—her very human face—and then it warmed even more. But at the moment she needed to pay attention to her clan members. After ten minutes, a small handful of her clan had turned to human. Sabrina instructed them on how to turn back to their demon forms while Lela went to stand next to Sergei.

"You look amazing! Congrats on mastering your human form."

"Thank you. But you weren't supposed to see this."

"Why not?"

"Because we want it to be a surprise. We're hoping to train all the immigrants to change into their human form prior to coming to earth. And other clan members decided they want to learn now as well." Lela leaned closer and whispered, "Can you keep a secret?"

"Absolutely. I can't wait to see Aleksei's face."

"Are you helping with supplies again? Sabrina said we're going to have a centralized location now."

"We are. I decided it would be easier to manage."

"You're officially managing this project?"

With a brief frown, Sergei said, "Not officially. You aren't the only one keeping a secret. Aleksei has a lot on his plate right now with the immigration in less than two weeks, earth time."

"Well, you're doing a wonderful job of it." She pointed to the bag at his feet. "What did you bring?"

"More books. Kyle said you want more."

"I do. We're going to distribute them to the five villages to help start acclimating the demons to earth."

"I'm impressed. What a great idea."

Sabrina walked up beside them. "See, Lela? Just what I told her, Sergei. She's a natural at this. When we get to earth, I'm going to have her talk to Aleksei about helping with the immigration."

Lela ducked her head at their praise. It was a lot to take in, along with everything else happening around her.

Sabrina smiled. "Why don't you two take a break? I'll keep working with those who want to try again."

"Are you sure?"

"Absolutely. Go catch up."

Lela led Sergei to the edge of her village overlooking the crystal caves. The red rocks had always fascinated Lela as a child, because they seemed to glow from within. Whenever she was upset or anxious, she would go to the caves and sit among the red crystals while they pulsed in a rhythm all their own.

Lela sat down on a felled tree, beckoning for Sergei to join her. He sat down slowly, taking his surroundings in with a slack jaw.

"This is incredible."

"It is. It's one of my favorite places in the realm. It absolutely teems with energy."

Sergi nodded. "It does. It feels like static electricity running across my skin."

"I'm glad you came to the realm again, Sergei. I enjoy spending time with you."

He took off the bag he carried on his back and opened it. "I brought you some more pictures from earth."

Lela held out her hand and he gave her the stack of pictures. "These aren't in a book."

"No. I took them."

Her eyes widened as she looked back down at the top photo. "How?"

"With a machine called a camera. It lets you capture different things in the world to share with others."

She moved from picture to picture. Unlike the books he had brought her, these pictures were much more than pictures of nature. They showed people and places she would never have imagined before. "These are wonderful. You are gifted." She studied a picture of a small girl standing in a field of purple flowers, wonder shining on her face. "I can feel what she is feeling."

Sergei smiled. "Her name is Claire. I met her in a place called Provence, where her family runs a lavender farm. Those are the purple flowers you see in the fields. Even though she has spent her entire life in these fields, when their blooming starts, she runs out into the middle and breathes in the fragrance."

"Thank you for sharing your world with me."

"It will be your world, too, before you know it. I know Sabrina mentioned that she was going to talk to Aleksei about you helping with the immigration. Is that what you want to do?"

Lela thought for a moment before responding. "I definitely want to help the clans successfully live on earth. I think now that the realm isn't being treated like a prison, the clans here are anxious to learn about their future home. If I'm allowed to help make the transition easier, I want to."

"I don't think Aleksei will have a problem with bringing you on to help, especially if you can help speed up the realm demons' acclimation to earth."

She looked at several more pictures while Sergei explained about Africa. She thought the elephant was amazing, until he showed her a giraffe with its baby, and then a lion on a rock, basking in the sun. "Can you talk to them?"

Sergei smiled. "You can talk to them, but they wouldn't understand you. And if you got close enough to a lion, you would probably want to ask him not to eat you."

Lela's mouth dropped open.

"These animals are wild. There are some that are much smaller, like the cats and dogs that live with humans. A cat is a miniature version of a lion."

"I'd like to meet a cat someday."

He chuckled. "That can definitely be arranged."

"Did I say something funny?"

"No, you said something delightful. I can't wait to see your face when you see some of this stuff in person." He held up his hand. "And before you ask, you will not be getting close to wild animals."

"Your home will be close to me?"

His smile dimmed slightly. "I travel a lot, so I don't have a home. But I'll be staying for a few more weeks after you arrive."

"I would like that very much." And she would, but she couldn't deny the tightening in her chest when she thought about him leaving. She looked down at the photos again to hide her disappointment.

Sergei cleared his throat. "I saw the elder touch you earlier. Did he hurt you?"

"No. Sabrina has been teaching me how to control my powers."

"So you can touch others now?"

Her cheeks heated when she looked up into his intense, golden-brown eyes. "I still am hesitant, but I hope that soon I'll be able to touch others without fear."

They turned back to the photos, and Lela lost herself in Sergei's stories. Her heart sped up as she listened to his deep voice. She was developing feelings for him, but she could never compete with what the world had to offer Sergei. His pictures were a testament to that.

A week after Sergei's previous visit, Lela and Sabrina traveled to the in-between to check on how Naya was doing with her pregnancy. She was six and a half months along, and definitely showing. Naya still had not told Aleksei the truth, and Sabrina had decided to try and nudge a reason out of her today. Because of that, Lela planned to stay outside the hut while they had their conversation.

After several minutes, the hut door opened up to a grim-looking Sabrina.

"What's wrong?" Lela asked as Marrick carried Naya outside.

"Naya's having trouble with the baby. She's having early contractions. We're taking her to earth."

Lela's heart pounded while she watched a portal form to take them to earth. The three of them stepped through the light, only to have it close moments later.

Lela stared at the empty space in front of her. With the time difference, she might not hear from them for days.

What would Aleksei think when he saw Naya? According to Sabrina and Sergei, only six weeks had passed on earth since Aleksei went home.

Sabrina was a good doctor. If anyone could help Naya and her baby, she could. And Sergei would be there for his brother.

Sergei and Misha stood outside the conference room, waiting for the meeting to end. Boris had petitioned the Shamat elders to change the rule of clan succession so Aleksei could become the leader even though Misha had stronger powers. The elders had agreed to meet today to discuss it. A few minutes ago Aleksei was called into the room as well.

"Do you think this will take long?" Sergei asked.

Misha shrugged. "It might. Father is asking them to change laws that have been part of our clan for centuries."

"Do you think they'll deny him the leadership?" Sergei couldn't imagine what that would do to Aleksei if it happened.

"Fates, I hope not."

The door flew open, and a fierce-looking Aleksei strode out of the room.

"How did it go?" Misha asked.

"They were willing to remove the stipulation that the one with stronger powers should rule."

"That's great!" Misha said.

"Until they told me I couldn't mate with Naya and rule."

"What?" Sergei and Misha blurted at the same time.

"They don't want a child with Pavel blood ruling the clan."

"And what did you say?" Misha asked.

"I told them in that case I wouldn't rule, and that they could ask one of you, or have an election."

"Holy shit," Sergei swore. "I'm surprised they didn't all have heart attacks."

"I didn't wait around to find out."

Misha placed his hand on Aleksei's shoulder. "Are you sure about this? You'd be giving up everything you've worked for most of your life."

"Not everything. I'm going to try to win Naya back, if I can convince her to give me a chance now that I won't be ruling. After we finish the realm immigration, I'll do what she wants to do. Go where she wants to go."

"Who are you, and what have you done to my brother?" Misha said.

"How many times have you told me to get the stick out of my ass?" Aleksei asked.

"Actually, that was Kyle."

"Well, don't tell her I said this, but she was right."

"I heard that," Kyle said as she appeared from around the corner.

"How long have you been listening?" Aleksei said.

"Long enough to hear you've finally come to your senses, brother."

A guard jogged down the hall toward them.

"What's wrong?" Aleksei asked.

"An unscheduled portal just opened in the compound."

"Are we being attacked?" Misha asked.

"No," the security guard said. "It is Marrick, Naya, and Doctor Miller. Marrick was carrying Naya."

"Where are they now?" Aleksei demanded.

"They went to the infirmary."

Aleksei bolted down the hall before the guard could say anything else. Sergei followed, with Misha and Kyle running alongside him. If anything happened to Naya, his brother would never forgive himself.

Sergei prayed that Naya would be okay. She had to be.

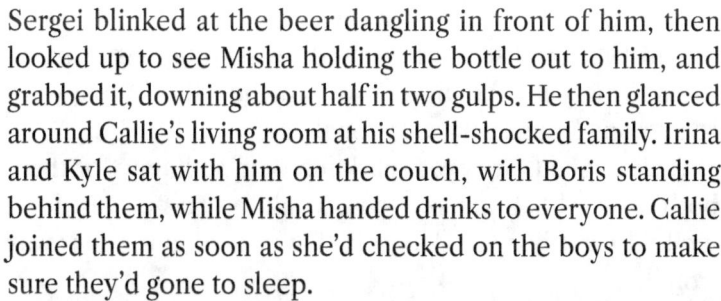

Sergei blinked at the beer dangling in front of him, then looked up to see Misha holding the bottle out to him, and grabbed it, downing about half in two gulps. He then glanced around Callie's living room at his shell-shocked family. Irina and Kyle sat with him on the couch, with Boris standing behind them, while Misha handed drinks to everyone. Callie joined them as soon as she'd checked on the boys to make sure they'd gone to sleep.

"I can't believe Aleksei is going to be a father," Sergei blurted.

Misha grinned. "Did you see his face? Priceless. Thank God Sabrina was able to stop the premature labor and Naya and the baby are going to be fine."

Kyle chuckled. "A secret demon baby! It couldn't have happened to a nicer male."

Boris slapped Misha on the back. "This has been one of the best days of my life. First, Aleksei meets with the elder council and tells them he's going to fight for Naya and they can either accept her as his mate, or they can find another successor for clan leader." He grinned at Misha and Sergei. "He pointed out that you were both available for the job. Then he left the room without a backward glance. You should have heard the elders sputter."

The last thing Sergei wanted was to be considered for clan leader, but he didn't have a chance to say anything before the guard showed up.

Boris continued after pouring himself a drink. "His announcement and departure from the meeting were poetic, and I thought I couldn't be prouder of him—until he stood in that hospital room and told Naya he loved her and wanted to be with her, damn the consequences."

Irina chuckled. "And then he found out he was going to be a father. I have never seen him happier."

Sergei couldn't agree more. When the truth came out that she was pregnant, it was as if a light switch flipped on inside his brother. Aleksei had insisted on staying with Naya at the infirmary for the night, and now the rest of them were recovering from a very emotional day.

Callie sighed, her eyes sparkling. "I'm so happy for them both. I heard Sabrina say Naya would be on bed rest for a while. I can't imagine Aleksei will want to be too far away from her."

Sergei nodded. "The immigration is in a week, so we all need to take on jobs to make sure it gets done. I'll come into the office tomorrow and help you and Doyle, if that would work."

The room went silent and he looked around at the shocked faces. "What? Did you honestly believe I wouldn't help out?"

Boris grinned from ear to ear. "No son, that's not it. But I've never seen you so determined before. You sounded a little bit like Aleksei just now."

Sergei grinned back at him. "I'll take that as a compliment."

Kyle narrowed her eyes at him. "You going to stick around for a while?"

"Kyle..." Misha said.

"I think it's a fair question. Since the rest of the family is too scared to ask, I'm going to put it out there."

Sergei paused before answering. She was a gutsy thing, for sure. "I'm planning to stay for a while, but I can't stay here permanently."

Irina held up her drink. "I want to toast this growing family. However far we travel, may we always find our way back home again."

"Hear, hear," Boris said as he clinked his bottle against Sergei's.

CHAPTER 14

Sergei walked into the office and found Callie typing frantically on her computer and talking into her headset at the same time. She had been like this the past three days he'd been helping her at the office while Aleksei stayed close to Naya.

"The Collins Street house is ready to go. Got it. That leaves the Ramsey Avenue house. Are you going there now?" She gestured for Sergei to take a seat next to her desk. "Good. Thanks, Doyle. I'll see you in a couple hours."

Callie hung up the phone and pulled the headset off, rubbing her ears. "I've been spending way too much time with that thing on. What do you have for me?"

"The warehouse is set to go, and there are medical supplies and toiletries and clothing set up there for the new arrivals. Lela mentioned the last time I was in the realm that Sabrina had already completed preliminary medical exams for the fifty who will be arriving, which should speed up the process once they come through the portal."

"Great," Callie said. "Do you have time to help with something else?"

"Of course."

"Doyle is checking the halfway houses to ensure that the construction is finished. Now we need to make sure all the various household items are stocked at the eight houses. I have a list here of what they will need. Can you work with your resources who help with the realm supplies and get the houses stocked before Wednesday?"

"Absolutely."

Callie picked up a couple sheets of paper and handed them to Sergei. "Here. Let me know if you have any questions."

Sergei perused the paper and stopped after a few rows of type. "Callie, this isn't a list of household items. This is a list of names, including their clan identification and powers."

"Oh shoot. Sorry about that." She rummaged through the pages on her desk. "Here you go."

"What is this for?" Sergei asked.

"It's the partial listing of realm demons for the newest immigration. Aleksei is having me prepare it so he can present it to the demon council. I'm not done with it yet."

Sergei flipped through the pages until he found Lela's name and saw that there was a blank space next to her powers. He barely managed not to crumple it in his fist. "When will Aleksei be back?"

"He's actually here now for a little bit. Is something wrong?"

"I need to discuss something with him." Sergei stood and went to Aleksei's office, opening the door without knocking.

Aleksei looked up from his computer and frowned. "Is something wrong?" He jerked to his feet. "Is it Naya?"

Sergei held up his hand. "Naya is fine. I need to talk to you about this." Sergei held up the sheets of paper.

"Why do you have that?"

Well, crap. He didn't want to get Callie in trouble. "I saw it on Callie's desk, and she told me what it's for. Why are you meeting with the Demon Council about this?"

Aleksei walked around his desk. "When the Council agreed to allow realm demons to come to earth, they asked for a few conditions. They wanted to know about them, including their clans and background."

"You mean their powers."

"Yes. It was a small price to pay in order for the immigration to occur. Why are you so interested in this?"

"Because Lela is on the list."

Aleksei sighed. "I have been struggling with that as well, Sergei. My first inclination is to lie and say she doesn't have any powers. But I don't think that's going to work."

"Why not?"

"Because the cat is out of the damn bag. That day you all came to the Kelmar camp to save me, I announced her power to practically the entire realm. I wish I could take it back, but I can't. By now the realm demons who weren't in attendance were told what happened by the ones who were. And we can't forget that we had realm demons from the demon trafficking ring who witnessed it as well. Since then, they've returned here, and I'm sure they've been telling other demons what happened."

"Damn it."

"Naya mentioned that with Sabrina's help, Lela has learned to control her powers, so she won't be as vulnerable by the time she arrives here on earth. Naya also mentioned that Lela is an energy empath. She can sense energy or the lack of energy in demons as well."

"Naya's been telling you quite a bit."

Aleksei shrugged. "She's been on bed rest for days, and I've been with her as much as possible. We've been doing a lot of talking." He stared at Sergei for a drawn-out moment. "While I appreciate your concern for Lela, I'm surprised you would get so worked up about it. You only saw her a couple of times while we were in the realm six weeks ago."

Sergei blew out a hard breath. "I actually saw her a couple days ago."

"What?! Explain."

"I've been delivering supplies to the realm."

Aleksei scowled. "Did you see Naya while you were there? Did you know she was pregnant?"

"Of course not, or I would have told you. I haven't seen her the last few times I've been to the realm."

Aleksei unclenched his fists. "Naya would have stayed away from you, the stubborn female. Why didn't I know about you going to the realm? Callie has said nothing to me when she reported the progress."

"Don't get mad at Callie. I asked her if I could help with anything, and I told her to keep it quiet."

Aleksei scowled. "Why did you tell her to keep your involvement a secret?"

"Because you would have said no."

Callie peeked in through the doorway. "He's right. You are extremely stubborn."

"Have you been listening at the door?" Aleksei demanded.

Callie's cheeks pinkened. "Yes. Don't be mad at Sergei. He just wanted to help, and I needed it."

"I'm sorry if you've been overwhelmed. You should have told me."

Callie shook her head. "You didn't need more on your plate. And Sergei hasn't merely been delivering the items, he's established the entire distribution channel, both here and in the realm. Plus he jumped in the past few days and helped Doyle and me organize and set up everything for arrival day."

Aleksei's eyes widened. "Really?"

"Really," Callie said, before shutting the door and leaving them alone in the office.

Sergei set the papers he held on the desk. "I know I'm the last person you want helping you, but I needed to do something. Until a few days ago, you were working yourself to death. Now, thanks to Naya, you don't look like you're walking around with your heart ripped out of your chest anymore. And on top of that, you've got your secret demon baby to get ready for."

Aleksei's eyes narrowed on him. "Stop calling it my secret demon baby. Kyle started that nonsense, and it needs to stop."

"I'm sorry if you're pissed off that I got involved."

Aleksei sighed. "I'm not mad because you did it. I'm mad because you think you're the last person I would want helping me. Honestly? The *last* person? Holy Fates, Sergei, how did we end up in this place?"

"I don't know. I couldn't stay here feeling like a disappointment to you and Father, and you were pretty vocal about it the last time I was home."

"You're right. I was pissed at you then. I felt like you had checked out on this family and were finding excuses to stay away."

"Full disclosure? I *was* finding excuses to stay away. I can't live up to your expectations."

Aleksei grimaced. "Nobody's asking you to live up to our expectations. You just have to live up to your own."

Sergei paused. Aleksei made it sound so simple.

"I'm going to be a father, Sergei. Which means you're going to be an uncle. I'm excited and petrified at the same time. I need you to be a part of my son or daughter's life, to be part of my life again. Do you think you can do that?"

Sergei nodded, since he was having trouble thinking what to say. But he couldn't tell Aleksei the crux of his problem. For years he'd believed they were ashamed of him.

But after his recent conversations with both Boris and Aleksei, he couldn't use that as an excuse anymore. He was the one who didn't feel worthy of his family, which meant *he* was the one who had to suck it up and get past it.

Easier said than done.

CHAPTER 15

Lela hugged her father, and he gasped before he squeezed her tight and then released her. "I am so proud of you. Enjoy your adventure, but remember, I expect you to visit me regularly."

She blinked away tears. "Absolutely. I want to help with the immigration, so it will give me an excuse to come see you more often."

He gave her one more bear hug before melting into the large crowd who had come to say goodbye to the fifty realm demons heading to earth. She smiled at the group. Over the past month, every one of them had mastered their human form, and had all changed in preparation for their journey.

Marrick stepped forward and activated the portal, the air vibrating with energy until a large, glowing doorway appeared. He gestured to the group to start walking, and Lela waved at her father one more time before stepping into the light.

A tightness in her chest made it hard to breathe, but before she could panic, she entered the largest room she had ever seen.

"Welcome to earth," Sabrina called out to the group as they clustered together, craning their necks to take in their surroundings. Sabrina had told her they would be arriving in what was called a warehouse, since it would be big enough for everyone.

Aleksei stood next to Sabrina, gaping, until she jabbed him in the ribs with her elbow.

He jumped up on a box and grinned down at them. "What a surprise to see you all in human form! That's wonderful, and will help speed up your acclimation to earth that much faster. We are so happy you're here.

"Normally, the first step would be to have a medical examination. However, Doctor Miller explained that you all had a preliminary exam while she was in the realm. So instead of starting there, we'll have you move over to the five clan tables against the wall, and we'll introduce you to your mentors. They'll help teach you about earth and answer your questions. Welcome, everyone!"

Lela looked over to the tables Aleksei had pointed out, and saw that each one was manned by a different clan member in demon form. She located the Kelmar table and went toward it.

After a few moments, all the immigrants stood in lines, chattering with each other in their excitement.

"Welcome."

Lela's heart lifted. She knew that voice. Smiling, she turned to face Sergei. "Hello."

He smiled back at her. "It's good to see you. He looked around at the rest of the demons. "I'm impressed. You all turned into your human form."

"Yes. It was wonderful to see Aleksei's face."

"My brother doesn't get surprised that often. Although this past week he's had plenty of surprises."

Marrick had explained to Lela what happened between Naya and Aleksei. "I understand he took the news of impending fatherhood quite well."

"He's a new person. I'm very happy for him. How are you feeling right now? Nervous?"

"A little bit. I'm hoping my mentor and I will get along. Do you know who my mentor will be?"

Sergei shook his head. "No. I've been helping out with other things this week. I didn't realize that there were mentors, or I would have found out for you."

Sergei's grandmother joined them. "Maybe I can help. I know who your mentor is—me."

Lela beamed. "I would be honored to have you teach me about earth."

"The honor is all mine. The only stipulation is that Boris doesn't like me to leave the compound very often, so you're going to stay with me instead of one of the halfway houses." She turned to Sergei. "Which means you're getting kicked out of my guest room. Your father is offering you a room at his house since you've decided to stick around for a while. Does that work for both of you?"

Lela and Sergei both nodded.

"Excellent! Let's get Lela checked in so we can get her settled in at home. This is going to be great. I can't wait to teach you about earth."

Lela nodded again, since words escaped her. Minutes on earth, and she was already overwhelmed. But then Sergei winked at her, and that small, secret, friendly gesture relaxed her. She would make this work. She was in a new world with new opportunities.

Lela wouldn't let fear stop her.

A few hours later, she sat on the soft seat Irina called a couch and took a deep breath. Irina's hut—no, house—boggled Lela's mind. With the flip of a switch, Irina created a fire to cook with. So many things, including lights that were powered by something called electricity. But Lela's favorite room was the bathing room. There was a waterfall in that room—a warm one, that she could bathe in!

Irina had patiently shown Lela the house, explaining everything to her. A few minutes ago, Irina took a hard look at Lela's face and told her to sit on the couch and relax for a few minutes. And Lela didn't argue with her.

She couldn't learn everything in one day.

A bell rang, and Lela sat bolt upright. Irina hurried through the room holding up her hands. "That noise is the door-bell. It alerts me when someone is coming to visit." She disappeared down the hall, and moments later Lela heard Sabrina's voice.

"I came to say hi and see how you're doing," Sabrina said as she joined Lela in the living room.

"I'm fine. Everything is great."

Irina laughed. "She's sweet, but she's also lying. I showed her just about everything in the house and overwhelmed her. She was getting a little pale, so I told her to take it easy for a while. I'll let you two catch up while I make dinner."

Lela cringed. "I hope Irina isn't upset with me."

Sabrina sat down next to her. "Irina's fine. She's a strong female who is well aware of the fact that this is a huge adjustment for you."

"This house..."

"Is unlike anything you could have imagined, I know. Every day will get easier as you see and experience new things. The books helped prepare you somewhat, but the reality of earth is something else."

"I can't wait to try the shower."

Sabrina laughed. "That truly is a wonderful invention. You will also love Irina's food. She is a very good cook." She looked Lela up and down. "Do you feel in control of your energy here?"

"Yes. I still can control the flow, and have pulled it to its safe place until I get used to being on earth."

"That's a good idea. I'm so happy you're here, Lela. Do you have any questions or concerns I can help you with?"

"I'm sure I do, but right now the words won't come."

Sabrina smiled. "I understand. I'll check in on you tomorrow as well. Once you get settled, you can decide if you still want to work with the immigration, or if something else sparks your interest."

"I want to help with the immigration. I can always do something else once all the realm demons who want to come to earth are here."

"I figured you'd say that. I'll see about getting you some time with Aleksei." Sabrina stood. "I meant it when I said I'm glad you're here. I consider you a friend now, and anything I can do to help you get settled, please let me know."

Joy bubbled in Lela's chest. Not only was she starting a new life, but she was also forming new friendships. And, as her father said, today was just the beginning of her adventure.

━━◆○◆━━

Sergei stood in front of his grandmother's house and tried to decide if he should knock. It had only been a few hours since Irina took Lela to her house, and Sergei probably shouldn't bother them today. His brain knew this, but something in his gut made him march up onto the porch.

Again he hesitated. He hopped off the front porch and went around to the back door leading to the kitchen. If he knew his grandmother, she would be in there cooking up a feast for Lela. He peeked through the glass window and saw his grandmother standing at the counter chopping vegetables. He knocked lightly on the door, and she tipped her head, inviting him to come inside.

"Hello, Sergei. What a surprise to see you here," his grandmother said, not sounding surprised at all, although she did give him a big smile.

"I was out for a walk and decided to check in to see how Lela is doing." He almost cringed at how flimsy that sounded, but there was no going back now. "Where is she?"

"She's napping on the couch."

Sergei frowned. "Is she sick? I can go get Sabrina—"

Irina held up her hand. "She's not sick. I think I might have overwhelmed her a little bit with everything I was trying to teach her. I made a cup of chamomile tea and told her to relax, and it worked better than a sedative. As soon as I'm done chopping these vegetables for the salad, dinner will be ready. Can you carry the rolls and butter into the dining room?"

Sergei did, and arranged the food on her dining room table. A table that was set for three people.

"Are you expecting someone else for dinner?"

Irina winked at him. "I figured *someone* might show up. Will you go wake her?"

Sergei walked slowly into the living room. Lela was curled up on one end of the couch, and she looked so peaceful, he hated to wake her. He took a step closer and studied her face. A light dusting of freckles dotted her nose.

"Are you going to wake her up or stare at her all day?" Irina whispered from the archway leading to the dining room.

Sergei glared at his grandmother, who chuckled as she returned to the kitchen.

"Lela," he said softly. When she didn't move, he raised his voice. "Lela. It's time to get up."

Her eyes opened slowly, and she looked up at him, confusion turning to recognition as she gave him a drowsy smile.

The look was like a kick to the gut. Was that the way she looked when she woke up in the morning? He took a deep breath and moved a step back. He should *not* be thinking about how she looked in bed. He needed to control himself.

"Hello," she said, sitting up.

"Hello yourself. I understand Grandmother already overwhelmed you."

Pink tinged her cheeks before she responded. "Just a little bit, but I can take it."

"I know you can. Grandmother has dinner ready. Do you mind if I join you?"

Her eyes lit up. "That would be wonderful."

Again with a kick to the gut. He was in trouble. But that didn't stop him from holding out his hand to help her off the couch. Her fingers gripped his lightly, and he hesitated before letting her go.

When they joined his grandmother in the kitchen, she greeted them with a twinkle in her eye. She was up to something. But when was his grandmother not up to something? She ladled soup into bowls, and they carried them to the dining room.

"I hope you like the soup. I learned when Naya stayed with me to introduce new foods slowly. This soup should be similar to what you've made in the realm. I also made a salad and rolls." Irina picked up a roll and tore it in half, dipping it into the broth. "This is the way I like to eat it."

Lela reached for her spoon and took a small sip of the broth, her eyes widening. "This is delicious, and you're right, it reminds me of our vegetables at home."

"Excellent. Dig in."

They ate in silence for a few moments, until Irina spoke. "Have all the new arrivals settled at the halfway houses?"

"Yes." Sergei reached for a roll. "Everyone is settled, and the mentors are spending the day with them. So far we haven't run into any issues."

"You seem to be very involved with the immigration," Lela said.

Sergei swallowed before answering. "Aleksei's been taking care of Naya, so the whole family chipped in to help. We want to make sure this immigration goes smoothly."

"How is Naya doing?" Lela asked.

"I visited with her yesterday," Irina said. "She's on bed rest, which she's having a tough time with, and she's hoping Sabrina will agree to let her get up soon."

"And Aleksei seems well."

Irina beamed. "He is a changed demon. I'm so happy for him, but his overprotectiveness is in full swing right now. He won't let Naya lift a finger, which is contributing to her cabin fever."

Sergei chuckled. "Cut the male some slack. He just found out he's going to be a dad, and confessed his feelings for her in front of our family. He's allowed to be a little overprotective."

Irina nodded. "You're correct. I will cut him some slack."

Lela set down her spoon. "When Aleksei isn't so busy, I would like to talk to him about helping with the immigration."

"That's wonderful," Irina said. "He can definitely use more help. I'll call him and set up an appointment for you tomorrow. Unless that is too soon?"

"No. I want to feel useful."

Sergei was awed by her selflessness. She just got to earth and already wanted to contribute.

Irina gathered the dishes, and both he and Lela carried everything to the kitchen, loaded the dishwasher, and put away the leftovers. Lela's eyes widened when the refrigerator opened, and she held her hand inside, feeling the cold air.

Irina shooed them toward the dining room. "You two go sit down. I'll bring the dessert in a minute."

When they sat, Sergei smiled at her, suddenly at a loss for what to say.

"You're looking at me strangely."

He straightened. "What?"

"Just now. You looked at me like you were trying to figure something out. You had the same look on your face when I said I want to help with the immigration."

"To be honest, I'm in awe of you. Your willingness to help immediately, even though you just got here, is amazing."

She shrugged. "I don't think I'm doing anything special. I need to feel useful. If the earth clans are willing to let us come here, shouldn't we be willing to help as well?"

Damn. It wasn't only her attitude and willingness that made her amazing. *She* was amazing. Period. And the more time he spent with her, the more she got under his skin. He was in trouble. This would never work. He needed to travel the world, and didn't want to be tied down. She needed a sense of family and permanence.

She sat up straighter when Irina walked in with the ice cream sundaes. Lela tasted the whipped cream, and, with big eyes and a cute grin, dipped her spoon in for a second taste.

Yep, he was in trouble, with a capital T.

CHAPTER 16

The next morning, Lela followed Irina down a long hall to a glass door. Irina winked at her before opening the door and leading her inside.

Lela came to a quick stop, taking in her surroundings. A blond human female sat poking her fingers on a slim silver box. A demon male paced in the corner of the room talking to himself. He had something black sticking out of his ear that led down to his mouth. Was he in pain? Did he need help?

Irina turned around when she realized Lela wasn't following her. She walked back and patted her arm. "That's Doyle, and he's not talking to himself. That thing you see sticking out of his ear is called a Bluetooth. It allows him to have conversations with people over long distances."

"Magic?" Lela whispered.

"Technology. Which some would call magic. Callie is typing on a computer. I'll explain some of this to you later, okay?"

"Okay."

The human female stood and smiled. "It's good to finally meet you, Lela. I'm Callie. I work with Aleksei, and he's expecting you."

Callie headed toward the back wall, and Lela glanced back at Irina, who was settled comfortably in a chair against a different wall.

"Go on, dear. You're more than ready to meet Aleksei on your own and tell him your ideas."

Lela swallowed hard before following Callie. She had expected Irina to be with her, but it wasn't like she didn't already know Aleksei. She hoped he would find merit in her ideas. Sabrina did. Callie knocked and then opened the door and beckoned for Lela to enter.

Aleksei stood and walked over to her. "Lela, it is so good to see you. I'm sorry I didn't get to spend any time with you yesterday, but it was a little busy."

"You don't have to apologize. Thank you for meeting me."

"Gladly. I understand from Sabrina that it was your idea to teach the arriving demons how to change into their human form before they left the realm."

"Yes. Sabrina volunteered to teach me how to do it, and I asked her to teach the others as well. I think I also have an idea for how to bring the realm demons to earth faster."

"That is my biggest concern as well. So much time passes in the realm compared to here, that we're at a disadvantage."

Lela nodded. "Yes, which is why I think we should start training everyone while they're in the realm. We have plenty of time there. Sabrina helped me learn about my new home before I came here, and the books Sergei brought about earth were distributed to the clans as well. We can help train the realm demons before they come to earth, so they're ready to go when they arrive. Then you wouldn't have to spend so much time here getting them settled. Plus, it will give them something to work toward while they wait for their turn."

Aleksei gaped at her, and her heart thumped so hard she could feel it in her throat. Had she overstepped?

A smile lit his face. "Lela. That is a great idea. I think you're on to something. I would hug you right now if I could."

"Let's try a handshake instead."

He reached out, and she placed her hand in his...and they shook! How wonderful that she could do something as simple as shake hands without cringing.

Aleksei flung open his office door. "Doyle! Callie! Come in here."

Both came running into Aleksei's office. Irina stood in the doorway.

"Lela has come up with an amazing idea." He turned to her. "You explain it to them."

She smiled as she repeated what she said to Aleksei.

Callie applauded. "That's it! It's perfect! We need someone to lead the effort."

Aleksei turned to Lela. "I think I'm looking at her."

"What?" Lela gasped.

"Who better than the person who experienced it firsthand and came up with the idea? Do you want to be a part of the immigration process?"

"Yes, but I'm new to your world. I don't know if I can do this on my own."

"We won't let you struggle, Lela. For right now, you can give us ideas of what to do in the realm as you learn here. Since Sergei is going to be here awhile longer, I'll have him work on getting the right supplies for you."

Lela took a breath. "I would like that very much. I also wonder if we might be able to recruit some of the mentors to go to the realm to train. A week away from earth would be a month in the realm."

Aleksei threw his head back, laughing. "Lela, you are a godsend. Welcome to the team."

Lela walked out of the immigration offices alongside Irina, and then stopped in the hall.

"What just happened?"

"You were sucked in by Aleksei. He's a natural."

"I wanted to help..."

"But you didn't think it meant leading the project. Don't fret, sweetie. In less than a day you've already suggested things that will improve the process dramatically. And with Sergei's help, you'll get up to speed in no time."

"Is Sergei really going to stay here for a while?" Lela asked as they opened the exterior door.

Irina looked at her for a long moment. "That's what he said the other day when Kyle questioned him."

"Kyle?"

"She works with Misha. You'll meet her soon. She saved Misha's life, and he adopted her into the family. She's the one who stood up to the Demon Council and petitioned for the realm demons to be allowed to come to earth."

Lela jerked to a stop. "She's the one? I can't wait to meet her."

"Let's get home, and I'll make lunch and teach you some more things, hopefully without overwhelming you this time."

Lela grinned. "I'm ready."

"Yes, you are, dear. Of that I have no doubt."

———◆○◆———

Lela never thought she could be both exhausted and exhilarated at the same time—until she came to earth, that is. The last couple of days had been all about experiencing new things.

Tonight she was going to Callie's house for a barbecue. Why they would want to roast meat over a fire pit when they had the magical stoves in their kitchens was beyond Lela, but she wasn't going to argue. She especially looked forward to meeting the twins. Lela had heard several stories about them from Irina.

And Sergei would be there as well. At least that's what Irina told her, more than once. Lela hoped Irina wasn't getting forgetful. Up to this point she had seemed to be a very sharp-witted female.

They walked up to a pretty gray one-story house. Lela knocked on the door since Irina was carrying a plate of something called peanut butter brownies. Apparently they were a favorite of the twins.

The door opened and Callie greeted them with a big smile. "I'm so glad you could come." She stepped back to invite them inside.

"Thank you for inviting me to your barbecue," Lela said.

Callie led them to the kitchen, chatting as she went. "We've been lucky September has been warm so far. The twins are spending every moment they can outside."

Callie stirred something on the stove before turning off the flame.

"Irina, I see you brought the boys' favorite. You're certainly spoiling them."

Irina chuckled. "It's not hard to do."

"Misha and Sergei are out taking care of the grill, and the boys are playing."

Lela wasn't sure exactly what a grill was, but she would find out soon enough. "I'd love to meet your sons."

"Go introduce them, Callie," Irina said. "I'll start plating the side dishes."

Callie nodded before opening the door that led to the backyard. Misha and Sergei had their backs to them and were looking down at a large metal box that had smoke wafting up over searing meat.

"How's it look?" Callie asked, causing both men to turn.

"The burgers are almost done," Misha said. "It's good to see you again, Lela."

Lela smiled. "You too."

Sergei walked over to her. "I'm glad you came tonight."

"I wanted to experience my first barbeque and meet the twins."

She glanced out into the yard—and paused, her eyes widening. What was *that*?

Sergei laughed. "You should see your face. I had almost the same reaction when I saw it for the first time."

"What is it?"

"That is what's known far and wide as a premium playset." He pointed to the large wood and metal thing the boys were climbing on. "That part is a slide. The boys can go up the ladder, and then sit and slide down on their bottoms. There is also a rock wall to climb, and a ladder that goes up to a small house to the right. And of course there are swings and monkey bars."

Lela swallowed. "They have monkeys?"

"Not real monkeys. It's a series of metal rungs they can hang from."

Lela didn't know what to say, but she was saved from responding when Callie called to the twins.

"Boys! It's time for dinner."

The twins ran toward the back of the house and stopped next to their mom. They had light brown hair and green eyes that matched their mother's.

Callie touched each head as she introduced them. "Matty, Luke, this is Miss Lela. She's staying with Miss Irina for a while to learn about earth."

Matty smiled up at Lela. "You're from the realm."

Lela nodded. "I am. I'm from the Kelmar clan."

Both boys perked up.

"We're from your clan," Luke said.

Lela frowned slightly at his proclamation.

"The boys' father was Kelmar," Callie explained.

Lela's eyes widened for a second before she recovered. "That means that we're fellow clan members." She bowed slightly. "It's wonderful to meet you."

The boys bowed as well.

"You can sit by us," Luke said. "We'll tell you about earth, and you can tell us about the realm."

"I'd like that very much."

Callie sent the boys inside to wash their hands just as Aleksei walked around the side of the house.

"Glad you could make it, Aleksei," Misha said.

"Thanks for inviting me, but I can't stay too long. I'm going to eat a burger and then take a plate back to Naya."

"I'm surprised you left her at all," Sergei said.

Aleksei mumbled something under his breath.

"What was that, dear?" Irina asked.

Aleksei frowned. "I said, she kicked me out for a while. Said I was hovering and she couldn't stand it anymore."

Misha laughed—until Callie elbowed him.

"It's not funny," Aleksei said. "I only want to keep her and the baby safe."

"Of course you do," Callie said, glaring at Misha. "But you have to remember that Naya is used to taking care of herself."

Irina chimed in. "She's right, Aleksei. Naya still needs to feel in control, and if you won't let her do anything, she's going to lash out."

He blew out a breath. "Got it." He turned to Lela. "How are things going for you? Is Grandmother being a good mentor, or do I need to get you a new one?"

Lela blinked at his question, until she looked up into his dancing eyes.

She grinned. "She is a wonderful mentor."

"Of course I am," Irina chimed in.

The boys practically tumbled through the back door in their rush to get outside. Callie and Irina brought out dishes of food, while Misha took the meat off the metal box and put it on a platter. Everyone sat down at the large table, and Lela gaped at the different dishes of food in front of her. Would she ever learn everything there was to know about her new home?

She looked across the table at Sergei. And would she ever understand her growing feelings for this male? Her brain knew he wasn't going to stay here long, but her heart didn't seem interested in heeding her brain's warning.

CHAPTER 17

Sergei had never imagined being usurped by seven-year-old twins. But the little demons were monopolizing Lela's time. He told himself he was being ridiculous. The boys were adorable. They had insisted on sitting on either side of Lela and helping her with her food, explaining everything to her.

Aleksei wasn't the only one who had hovering down to a science.

"Would you like some baked beans?" Luke asked Lela. "They are vegetables that grow in the ground. Momma puts spices and brown sugar on them and cooks them for a long time on the stove."

"They're good," Matty volunteered. "So's the potato salad. Naya said you have potatoes in the realm, but they're blue. You should try some potato salad too."

Lela beamed at them both. "Thank you so much for explaining everything to me."

The boy's chests seemed to puff up at that. Lela was snaring more males in her gorgeous and big-hearted web. Sergei's fork came to a stop in midair. Was that what she had done to him? If he was honest with himself, the answer would be yes.

Damn.

But the question was, did he really want to untangle himself from her? He watched her while she tipped her head back and laughed at something Matty said to her. The answer was no.

Damn it.

"Is everything okay, Sergei?" Irina asked.

He tore his gaze from Lela to look at his grandmother before nodding, even though everything was far from okay.

Irina gazed at him for a moment, eyebrows raised...in concern? With humor? What was she looking at?

His fork still hanging in midair.

He stuffed the food into his mouth and chewed, not tasting it. Quickly he set his fork down and drank some water to help him swallow, since the food sat like a lump in his throat.

The boys were trying to get Lela to try some pickles, and she was wrinkling her cute, delicately freckled nose up at the vinegar smell. He took another swig of water.

Before he could continue to make an ass of himself, his father appeared around the back of the house and waved to everyone.

"Sorry I'm late."

Callie smiled and beckoned to him. "We're just glad you could make it."

Boris sat down next to Misha and grabbed a plate. "I had to finish up some things at the office before I leave for my trip tomorrow."

"Where are you going this time?" Misha asked.

"New York. When I return, I've decided to throw a thank-you celebration for everyone who helped with the most recent immigration. My assistant is going to send out invitations to everyone for next Saturday for dinner." Boris looked down the table at Lela. "That includes you, too, Lela. Aleksei told me about your ideas to help the immigration. Welcome to the team."

Lela's cheeks pinkened before she smiled at Boris. "Thank you. Aleksei said the same thing to me. Now I know where he gets his charisma."

Boris grinned. "I keep telling him he's a chip off the old block."

Aleksei groaned, dropping his forehead to his hand and shaking his head.

"Mr. Boris," Matty spoke up. "Why are you calling Aleksei a chip? You need to explain things better for Miss Lela, too."

Boris chuckled. "You are absolutely correct, Matty. I'm sorry to have confused you. A chip off the old block is a saying that means Aleksei takes after me. That we are alike."

Matty looked over at Lela. "Does that make sense?"

"Yes. Thank you for asking for an explanation. I need to remember to do the same thing when I don't understand."

The rest of the meal was full of good food and laughter. Aleksei left first with a plate for Naya and a reminder from Irina not to hover.

Irina mentioned that she was tired, and Lela started to get up, but Irina shook her head. "Why don't you stay for a little while longer? Boris can escort me home, and Sergei can bring you home later...if that's okay with him?"

Sergei gave his grandmother a sharp look, and she smiled back sweetly, all innocence. Hah. "That's fine. I'll bring her home."

Irina and Boris said their good nights and left.

"Okay, if everyone grabs dishes and brings them into the house, we'll be done with the cleanup in a snap," Callie announced.

Misha, Sergei, Lela, and the twins followed Callie into the house with dishes, placing them on the counter and table.

"Can we go play outside, Momma?" Luke asked.

"Only for a couple more minutes. It's going to be dark soon, and we need to check your homework before you go to bed."

"Miss Lela, will you come with us?" Matty asked.

"Of course. I would like to examine your playset."

Sergei smiled as the boys each grabbed one of her hands and pulled her outside.

Callie giggled. "I think the boys are a bit smitten with Lela."

Sergei nodded. He couldn't blame them.

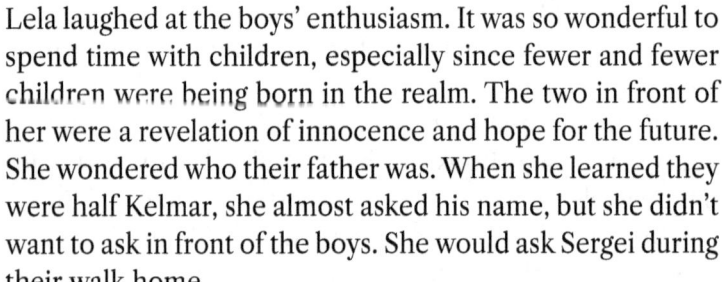

Lela laughed at the boys' enthusiasm. It was so wonderful to spend time with children, especially since fewer and fewer children were being born in the realm. The two in front of her were a revelation of innocence and hope for the future. She wondered who their father was. When she learned they were half Kelmar, she almost asked his name, but she didn't want to ask in front of the boys. She would ask Sergei during their walk home.

Her heart sped up. She would be walking home with Sergei. Alone. She wasn't sure why she was nervous. She had spent time alone with Sergei in the realm. What was different?

Her growing feelings, that's what.

She yanked herself out of her thoughts and watched the boys clamber over the playset. They climbed the ladder and went down the *slide*, as Sergei called it. She chuckled at their looks of glee.

"These are swings," Matty said as both boys sat down and pumped their legs while they moved back and forth, higher and higher.

Lela got woozy as their swinging increased.

"Watch, Miss Lela!" Luke called as the swing went forward very high, and he let go and flew through the air.

Lela's heart seized when Luke landed hard on his feet and then cried out as he tumbled to the ground.

Lela ran over to him and knelt, while Luke whimpered before starting to cry.

"Go get help, Matty," Lela said.

Matty tore into the house, and moments later Misha, Callie, and Sergei ran outside.

"What happened?" Misha got to them first.

"I'm so sorry," Lela said. "He was swinging, and he let go and flew through the air. I think he landed too hard on his feet."

"It's not your fault," Misha said as he reached for Luke.

"Don't move him, Mish!" Sergei commanded. "We need to figure out where he's hurt first."

Callie knelt near Luke's head. "Where does it hurt, baby?"

"My leg."

Lela checked him over, watching his energy flow through his body. He seemed fine, except for his ankle, where energy swirled haphazardly. "It's his right ankle."

Misha rolled up Luke's pants leg, and they could see his ankle was already starting to swell. "We need to get him to the infirmary."

"Give me your car keys," Sergei said, then took them and ran toward the front of the house.

Misha scooped Luke up, and they all rushed around the side of the house. By the time they got there, Sergei had the car running and all the car doors open. Matty crawled into the third-row seats without a word, even though he had tears in his big green eyes. Callie climbed into the back seat of the car, and Misha set Luke on her lap. Lela ran around the other side of the car and straightened out Luke's leg, holding it.

She hated to hear the whimper he made while she held his ankle. Callie looked over at her and blinked away tears as well. Sergei got back behind the wheel, with Misha in the front passenger seat, and they drove toward the infirmary. On the way, Misha spoke into the small device Irina had explained to Lela was a phone, and told someone they were on the way. He hung up a few moments later.

"We're in luck. Sabrina is still at the infirmary. She was finishing up some immigration paperwork."

Luke sucked in a hard breath between sobs. Callie leaned down and kissed his forehead while Lela examined his ankle again. More energy swirled in an almost angry pattern around his leg. She wanted to help. To soothe him somehow. Lela pushed a little bit of her own energy into his leg. Her hands warmed over his ankle. She kept doing it a little at a time, and Luke's energy started to calm down, and his sobs turned into whimpers.

She pushed more energy into him, and he stopped crying altogether. She looked up at his face, and he was staring at her with wide eyes.

She smiled at him, even though her heart beat frantically. Had she helped him? Or made it worse?

A minute later they pulled up to the infirmary. Sabrina was waiting at the door with a male and some sort of cot on wheels.

When the car stopped, Sabrina opened the back door and the male picked Luke up gingerly and laid him on the cot.

Everyone followed them into the building. While the male pushed Luke into a room, Sabrina stopped for a moment.

"Lela and Sergei, why don't you wait with Matty in the waiting room?"

Sergei nodded and reached for Matty's hand first, and then her hand, before leading them down the hall to a room with chairs.

Lela sat and held her arms out to Matty, who climbed into her lap and hid his face against her shoulder. "It's okay, Matty. Luke will be fine. Sabrina is taking good care of him."

He sniffled against her shoulder, and Sergei sat next to them and rubbed his hand up and down Matty's back. They sat for several minutes in silence.

"I should probably call Grandmother and Father and let them know what's going on."

Before she could respond, Misha walked into the room, took one look at Matty, and scooped him up into his arms.

Sergei and Lela stood up.

"Is Luke going to be okay?" Sergei asked.

Misha nodded, and looked at Lela for a moment before responding. "Yes. Why don't you three come back with me?"

Sergei reached for Lela's hand again and they followed Misha. Luke was propped up with pillows on the rolling cot with his right pant leg cut off. Callie and Sabrina stood on either side of the bed.

Misha turned Matty so he could see his brother. "Everything is okay, Matty. Luke is going to be fine."

Lela was shocked when she looked down at Luke's leg.

"His leg isn't swollen anymore, Sabrina," Sergei said. "What did you do?"

Sabrina shrugged. "I didn't do anything. The swelling has been going down the last few minutes. He had a bad sprain, but it looks like it's been healing for days instead of happening minutes ago."

"How?" Sergei asked.

"Luke, tell Sergei what you told us."

Luke actually grinned a little bit. "Miss Lela healed me."

Lela took a step back, and Sergei's hand tightened around hers, as if to stop her from running away.

Sabrina went over to her. "It's okay, Lela. Can you tell me what happened?"

"I looked inside him, the way I did when we were working with the patients in the realm, and I could see his energy was gathering around his ankle. I was holding it steady in the car, and he was in pain."

"What did you do?"

"I pushed some of my energy into his leg, and it seemed to calm his energy down, so I gave him some more." Lela stared at the shocked faces. "I just wanted to help. Did I do something wrong?"

Callie took a step and threw her arms around her. "Thank you for healing him."

Lela looked over Callie's shoulder at Sergei, who watched her closely. She hugged Callie back, and Sergei smiled and nodded.

Thirty minutes later, Sergei and Lela walked toward Irina's house. She kept pace with him as they strolled around the community center. He looked over at her and grinned.

"What?"

"You are amazing. After everyone taking from you for years, you were willing to give your energy to Luke."

"He was hurt. I wanted him to feel better."

"Like I said. Amazing." He stopped walking. "You feel okay, right? You don't feel weak again, do you?"

"No. I actually feel great. So great I'm not ready to return to Irina's yet. What if we stroll around the lake for a bit?"

"Sure."

She held out her hand to him, holding her breath at the same time. He hesitated for a brief moment before enveloping her hand with his. She let out her breath slowly as they walked over to the lake next to the community center.

Many shades of pink and gold highlighted the sky, and were reflected in the water as the sun slowly set. She was awestruck by the world she lived in now. And she'd only seen a tiny part of what earth had to offer.

"It's so beautiful," she said.

"Yes, it is."

She glanced over at him and realized he wasn't looking at the lake, but down at her.

"You're missing the sunset."

"I'm seeing it through your expression."

She followed her instincts and stood on tiptoe, kissing him quickly before backing away. Before she was able to escape, he grabbed her arms and gazed down at her.

Her heart pounded so hard she could feel it in her throat. Had she actually kissed him? She was so nervous, she hadn't been able to enjoy her first kiss—she could barely remember it now, and it had happened mere seconds ago.

Sergei leaned down and kissed her again. But this time it would not be something she forgot, especially when he nibbled at her bottom lip.

She gasped, and he pulled her closer to him as his tongue sought entry to her mouth. As he took control, she decided she'd been missing out on the wonder of kissing for far too long.

Groaning, she pressed up against him, and after a few seconds he pulled away from her mouth and rested his forehead against hers, blowing out a hard breath.

"Damn."

"Did I do something wrong?" she asked.

"You did the opposite of wrong."

"Then why did you stop?" she pushed. Who was this brave female living in her skin?

He lifted his head so she could see his face and his beautiful golden brown eyes, which seemed to grow darker as he stared at her.

"I stopped because I think we need to slow down a bit. If I'm not mistaken, that was your first kiss."

Heat rushed up her neck into her face, and she tried to turn away from him, but he rested his hands on her shoulders and stopped her.

"I obviously don't know what I'm doing," she said.

He squeezed her shoulders. "Trust me. You do know what you're doing. But I assume, since you couldn't let people touch you in the past, you haven't kissed anyone either."

"I haven't."

"Then we take this slow."

His hands ran down her arms and wrapped around hers before pulling her along the path leading to Irina's house.

"Irina will be wondering where you are. By now she has probably heard about what happened with Luke and will want to know all the details."

She nodded. "Very well. But I want to practice kissing another time."

He laughed. "I'll make a note of that."

Lela smiled. "You do that."

They ambled hand in hand to Irina's, and he left her on the doorstep, but not before they practiced one more time.

CHAPTER 18

Sergei had been summoned to Aleksei's office...or at least that's what it felt like. When he arrived, he found his brother sitting behind his desk, frowning and looking like the old, cranky Aleksei, before he and Naya got together.

"Is Naya okay?" Sergei asked.

"Yes, she's fine. We need to talk."

"About what?"

"Lela. Word has spread around the compound like wildfire. I understand she cured Luke."

"He wasn't dying, Aleksei. He had a sprained ankle. She sent some of her energy into his leg, and it brought the swelling down."

"You know how rumors grow around here. We need to make sure it doesn't get out of hand. Is Sabrina working with Lela on this?"

Sergei frowned. "It happened last night. I don't know what, if anything, they've talked about today."

"I don't want anyone trying to take advantage of Lela. She's just settling in on earth."

"I agree," Sergei said. "I'll let her know to be careful."

Aleksei nodded. "Good. While you're here, I want to discuss something else, too. I want you to be a part of the next meeting with the Demon Council."

Sergei almost groaned out loud. "You know that's not my thing, Aleksei."

"I get that, but I think the leaders need to hear what the distribution efforts in the realm have evolved into. You're the one responsible, so it makes sense to have you report on it. I'm going to have Lela speak as well."

Sergei frowned. "Do you think that's a good idea after what you just told me?"

"I think we need her to be there. We don't want to segregate her, because if we do that, others will speculate that we're hiding her for a reason. Besides, she wants to be a part of this. Even if I did suggest she sit on the sidelines, do you think she would listen?"

"No. But that doesn't mean I'm not going to protect her at this meeting. Council leaders or not, they will show her respect."

"Absolutely. It's a good thing you'll be there to talk, then. Right?"

"You are seriously twisted, brother. I think you could talk anyone into anything."

"No, that title belongs to Father."

Sergei wondered if it was the truth any longer. Aleksei convinced you to help by appealing to what you really cared about. Should it bother him that his brother had already realized that Lela was his Achilles heel?

———◆O◆———

Lela tapped her feet under the dining room table. Today she would be sitting in on a meeting with Aleksei, Callie, and Doyle while they updated the Demon Council about the newest immigration. Aleksei wanted her there while he explained the newest plan, which she had suggested.

She nibbled on the piece of toast Irina made for her after insisting she couldn't go to the meeting on an empty stomach. Lela disagreed. Her anxious stomach would be much better off empty than full.

"Stop fidgeting, dear. Everything is going to be fine."

"What if they don't like my ideas?"

"They'll love your ideas. Aleksei would never have you address the Demon Council if he didn't think your ideas have merit. He will be there to make sure everything goes smoothly. And Boris is calling in for it as well. He'll steer the conversation in the right direction if need be."

"You sound so sure of yourself."

"I'm sure of you, and sure of my son and grandson. Now finish that toast and drink a bit of the peppermint tea. It will calm your nervous stomach."

Lela choked down the rest of the toast before Irina pushed her out the door to the community center. Irina's house was so close to the building that Lela had very little time to collect her thoughts before arriving at the large meeting room.

She hesitated outside the door. Was she ready for this?

"You look like you're about to make a run for it."

She turned to find Sergei coming toward her. "I thought about it for a moment. Are you going to the meeting?" she asked, trying to keep the hope out of her voice.

"Yes. Aleksei can be very persuasive. He wants me to brief the Council about distributing supplies in the realm."

"You can also tell them about the plans to train the realm demons, too."

Sergei shook his head, face straight...until the right side of his mouth cocked up. "Oh, no, that's your job. I don't think Aleksei would appreciate us messing with his plan for the meeting."

Before Lela could try to convince him, a small female strode toward them. She had black hair with bright red streaks down the one side. Did other earthers have hair like that?

The female stopped and nodded to Sergei before turning to Lela. "Hello. I'd like to introduce myself. I'm Kyle. Aleksei told me how you came up with some amazing ideas to speed up and improve the immigration."

Lela blinked at her.

"Are you okay?" Sergei asked. "You look pale."

"I'm...f-fine. I can't believe I'm meeting you," Lela gushed.

Kyle glanced behind her, and then turned back Lela. "Are you talking to me?"

"Of course! If it wasn't for you, the immigration wouldn't be happening. You're famous in the realm. Thank you *so* much."

"You're welcome." Kyle's cheeks darkened. "I'm glad you're here and willing to help with the immigration."

"How could I not help my own?"

The three of them entered the room, and a dozen faces turned toward them. Lela's stomach tumbled with nerves again, but she took a deep breath to calm herself. What she was doing was important. If Kyle could convince the Council to let her people come to earth, Lela would play her part. Sergei rested his hand lightly on her back for a moment and smiled down at her. She could do this.

Aleksei got to his feet and introduced Lela and Sergei to everyone. Now, on top of a churning stomach, her head spun with all the names she had no hope of remembering.

Everyone took their seats, Sergei and Kyle on each side of her, which helped to calm her down.

A voice came out of nowhere, making Lela jump.

Sergei placed his hand on her arm. "That's Father. He's on the phone."

"Since I'm calling in, I'm going to let Aleksei lead the beginning of the meeting in my absence. Once we've had the updates on the immigration, we'll allow Aleksei and his team to leave before we begin our normal Council meeting."

Aleksei leaned forward. "As you know from our last status meeting, we successfully brought fifty realm demons to earth. Since then they have been assigned mentors and are acclimating to their new world."

The clan leader across from Lela spoke. "Has the violence and unrest calmed down in the realm?"

"Yes. Since we've been having discussions with the clan leaders, we have put new plans in place to make living in the realm more tolerable. I'm first going to have Sergei report to you about the new distribution systems he has established in the realm."

Sergei explained how the clans received the items they needed. The clan leaders peppered him with questions, but Sergei answered them all calmly. Lela was the one whose nerves started to jump. She was not eloquent like Aleksei, or straightforward like Sergei.

After a few more questions, Aleksei took over the conversation again. "Besides the distribution program, we've also initiated a new way to help speed up the immigration process. Lela is a new immigrant, and she suggested these ideas to us. I'm going to have her explain them to you."

All eyes turned to Lela, and she swallowed hard. She could do this. She had practiced with Irina the night before.

She outlined the plans for the Council, giving examples of what they had done with the recent immigration. She looked around at the faces and saw a combination of reactions—curiosity, disbelief, wonder, and a little bit of distrust thrown in. She honestly couldn't blame them for any of those responses. Hadn't the realm demons been just as leery?

She finished the points she wanted to make and asked if there were any questions. There were plenty of questions. Surprisingly, she didn't wilt, even when some of the questions from Council leaders felt more like an interrogation. Finally the last of the questions were asked and answered, and Aleksei thanked her.

"Yes, Lela, thank you." Boris said through the phone. "Do you have any questions you would like to ask the Council?"

Lela thought for a moment before speaking. "I would like to know how the Council works."

"The demon clans on earth each select a representative to be Council leader. They are individually responsible for voicing their clan's wishes, and, as a group, for coming together when there are issues that impact all demons," Boris replied, with a slight echo from the box that sat in the middle of the table. "They weigh in on the issues and come to a consensus on how things will be handled."

Lela nodded before realizing that Boris couldn't see her. "So when do the realm clans get a representative on the Council?"

Silence.

How could a room full of so many be so quiet?

She looked around the table at the shocked faces.

One of the leaders spoke up. "Why would we have a realm demon on the Council?"

Lela frowned. "Why wouldn't you?"

Another leader leaned forward and smiled slightly. "I think what he is trying to say is that realm demons are new to earth, and aren't yet knowledgeable about how things work here."

"But they are knowledgeable about how their clans work. If the Council is about voicing clan wishes and addressing problems that involve all demon clans, then you would need people from the actual clans to do that."

Kyle tapped her fingers on the table. "I agree. If we're bringing the realm here to live, we can't simply enforce our edicts on the clans without their buy-in."

Boris chimed in. "This is a subject we'll need to discuss as part of our Council meeting. Thank you, Aleksei, Sergei, and Lela, for updating us today on the immigration progress and process. I think I can speak for the Council when I say we're impressed with the huge strides you've been making."

Lela walked out of the room quickly, with Sergei, Aleksei, and Kyle right behind her. She practically ran outside.

"Lela, wait!" Sergei grabbed her arm to stop her. She stood on the sidewalk with the other three circling her.

"I'm sorry."

Sergei frowned. "For what?"

"For speaking up in there. I didn't have the right."

Aleksei chuckled. "You had every right, Lela. And what you said made perfect sense."

"Damn straight," Kyle said before rocking her shoulders back and forth as she turned in a circle.

"Is she ill?" Lela whispered to Sergei.

Sergei laughed. "No, she's doing a happy dance."

Lela would have to ask Irina later what a happy dance was, and if she should be doing them as well.

Kyle stopped and faced her. "You asked the right question in there, Lela. I'm embarrassed we didn't think of it ourselves. Integrating the realm with earth isn't only about clothes, and food, and all the things we're teaching you from books. It means including you as well. You can't be part of the new demon earth we plan to build if you aren't part of the decision-making process."

"Agreed," Aleksei said. "Not to mention that earthers, as you call us, need to learn from the realm as well."

She glanced over at Sergei, who had been mostly quiet through the exchange. "What do you think?"

"I think you're right. I also think you're remarkable."

His words warmed her heart, and heat traveled up her neck onto her face. His opinion meant the world to her, and that in itself made her nervous.

She couldn't let herself rely on Sergei. She had to be able to stand on her own in this new world. She hadn't been trying to forge a new path during the Council meeting, but rather she was asking what she thought was a straightforward, obvious question.

Earth was new to her, but the concepts of cooperation and inclusion were something that she would ensure her realm brothers and sisters benefitted from after a millennium of being discarded and ignored.

CHAPTER 19

Lela blinked at the females gathered in Aleksei's house. Sabrina had convinced her to go with her to visit Naya. What she hadn't told her was that Kyle and Callie would be there too.

She had been invited to a girl's night. And while she didn't know what it entailed exactly, it couldn't be any worse than attending the Council meeting. Or so she hoped.

They sat in chairs in the living room while Naya reclined on the couch. Tonight's food experiment was called pizza. Lela was fascinated by the circle of bread that had been cut into large triangles.

Kyle thrust a plate into Lela's hand before picking one up for herself. "How is the patient doing?"

Sabrina smiled. "If everything goes well, Naya will be off of bed rest by the weekend."

Naya rolled her eyes. "Thank you. I'd like my baby's father to be alive for the birth, but I'm going to hurt him soon if things don't change."

"Duly noted," Sabrina said.

"He carried me to the living room, even though I explained to him that I've been getting up to use the bathroom all by myself for days. But he wouldn't listen. I had to threaten him to get him to leave."

"He's worried about you," Callie said.

"I know, but I can take care of myself."

Callie took a sip of her drink. "We know you can take care of yourself, but isn't it nice to have someone ready to pick up the slack?"

Naya's frown softened. "Yes."

"Can we eat the pizza before it gets cold?" Kyle asked.

"Way to ruin the moment, Kyle. You've been hanging around with Misha too much. Worrying about the food," Sabrina said.

"Speaking about being with someone a lot. Lela has been spending a lot of time with Sergei," Callie said with a grin.

"They spent a lot of time together in the realm as well. Sergei is obviously smitten with you," Sabrina said.

"Smitten?"

"He likes you. A bunch."

"And I like him as well. He is kind, and smart, and beautiful. And he is a very good kisser."

Callie bounced in her chair with a big grin. "Yay! That's great."

Lela beamed at her enthusiasm. "I agree. He told me he wants to take things slow, but I have decided to seduce him. Can you tell me how it works here on earth?"

Kyle dropped her pizza on the floor with a thwack. "Crap. That was a perfectly good piece of pizza. Warn a girl the next time you're going to say something like that."

Naya laughed so hard she had to clutch her belly.

Kyle gaped at her. "Stop laughing so hard. You're pregnant."

Sabrina rolled her eyes. "She's not going to laugh the baby out of herself, Kyle."

"You don't know that."

"Actually, I do. I'm a doctor."

"Let's get back to Lela's question," Callie interrupted them.

"You can't tell Misha," Lela said to the petite human.

Callie winked. "I promise. Misha would tell Sergei for sure, so my lips are sealed."

"Or Aleksei," Lela said looking at Naya.

Naya held up her hands. "I won't say a thing. I think it's good that you're planning to seduce him. That's what I did with Aleksei."

Kyle grabbed her drink and took a large gulp of it. "TMI, Naya. I'm a little surprised to learn you had to instigate it. Aleksei seems to be quite the go-getter."

Naya grinned. "It didn't take much to get him to go."

"Obviously, Miz Preggers. I still can't believe you're having a surprise demon baby."

Sabrina chuckled. "Stop picking on Naya. Demons normally can sense their cycles. It's not her fault the portal jumps threw her body out of whack." Sabrina looked at Lela. "Which means we should make sure you have some contraceptives, since you plan to seduce Sergei. We don't know what the time difference between worlds has done to your cycle, either."

Lela nodded, even though she didn't know what contraceptives were, exactly.

"I'm jealous." Callie held up her hand. "Not about the pregnancy. The twins are enough to handle right now. I still haven't, well...you know...with Misha," Callie said.

Kyle smacked her hand against her forehead. "Oh, Mish is such a goober. I'm not surprised about that announcement at all."

Callie blew out a frustrated breath. "Between the immigration and the boys, we're never alone together."

A voice chimed in from the doorway. "So I'll watch the boys one night so you can seduce Misha."

Everyone turned to see Irina.

Callie blushed bright red. "Oh, Lord. How long have you been standing there?"

"Long enough to know we've got our work cut out for us."

"I'm sorry," Callie blurted.

"About what? Sweetie, I want my grandsons to be happy, and part of that naturally includes having sex. I always forget how uncomfortable humans are about discussing sex. It's a natural part of life. Why don't we plan for the twins to stay over with Lela and me after the dinner party Boris is throwing on Saturday? That'll give you plenty of alone time with Misha."

Callie perked up. "That'd be great. I've been planting some clues with him, but I think being subtle isn't working."

"I agree, dear. Misha needs the direct approach."

"Please don't tell me we have to do an intervention on him again," Kyle moaned.

Irina chuckled. "No, dear. I think Callie simply needs to be blunt with him. Can you do that?"

"Yes, ma'am."

"We mustn't forget about a plan for Lela," Naya said.

"I haven't forgotten," Irina said. "Boris is out of town, which means Sergei is alone at the house. I think we set up a romantic evening for Sergei, with dinner and whatever else develops. I'll take care of the menu. And you girls take care of Lela."

Sabrina rubbed her palms together and looked Lela up and down. "It's time for you to venture outside the compound anyway. How about we go shopping?"

Lela looked at Kyle. "Should I be scared?"

"Very."

Sabrina gave Kyle a friendly shove. "Don't listen to Kyle. She's a whiner when it comes to getting dressed up."

Irina chuckled. "This is going to be fun. Misha and Sergei will never know what hit them."

Lela frowned. "I have to hit Sergei with something?"

"It's a figure of speech. It means you're going to surprise him. It doesn't hurt to nudge my grandsons down the right path. Fate knows I've been trying to do that for centuries."

Lela smiled. "Happy to help." And she was. She wanted to let Sergei know how serious she was about her growing feelings for him. If she had to nudge him, then let the nudging begin.

Kyle hooted. "This family is insane."

Irina wrapped her arm around Kyle. "Then it makes perfect sense that you've been adopted into it. And the rest of you, too. I love my son and grandsons, but it's hard being the only female. Thank you all for being a part of this family."

Warmth filled Lela's heart. There were fewer and fewer females in the realm, so she never had the opportunity to form those bonds. She would embrace these newfound friendships with open arms. And with their help, she would convince Sergei to speed things up a bit.

***

Sergei entered the house and was greeted by an amazing smell. Had his father cut his business trip short? "Hello?"

When he walked into the kitchen, the delicious smell hit him full force. Something Italian, based on the mouthwatering aromas of basil and oregano. He was starving and couldn't wait to eat.

He pushed open the door to the dining room and jerked to a stop.

There would be no eating anytime soon. He was too busy choking on his own tongue. Lela stood in the dining room. She wore a green dress the color of emeralds, and her red hair hung in loose waves over her bare shoulders. The skirt stopped a couple of inches above her knees, and his stare traveled down her incredible legs to take in her cute bare feet with painted toenails. So unexpected, and yet so Lela.

He wanted to take her picture, and then he wanted to take her in his arms and taste her neck and other parts of her—

No. He needed to get a grip.

"You look incredible."

Her cheeks pinkened. "Thank you." She propped one bare foot over top of the other.

"I love your feet," he blurted. Where had his filter gone?

Her face flamed darker. "I tried to wear heels, but I need more practice in them."

"You look perfect."

She walked up to him.

He froze. "What's the occasion?"

"I want to spend some time with you. To thank you for all you've done for me." She stopped in front of him and tilted her head up to gaze into his eyes.

And now he was having trouble swallowing again.

"You're welcome," he said. He really needed to take a step back.

"I like you, Sergei. A lot. You promised me we could practice kissing."

"What happened to taking it slow?" he asked, his voice sounding rough on the last word.

"That was your idea, not mine." She placed her hands on his chest, and heat seemed to flow over him from her fingertips.

"I want to feel you, Sergei. Against me, inside me. I just want you."

Damnation. He sucked in a breath. This female was going to kill him. If this was what she was like before sex, what would she be like once she had sex?

"I..."

She placed her fingers on his lips. "I understand that you can't promise me anything, Sergei, and I'm not asking you to. But I've spent my whole life separated from others. I care about you, and I want you to be my first."

This is not a good idea, his brain screamed, but his body ignored him and leaned forward, capturing her lips. She moaned lightly. *Really not a good idea*, as his lips slid down her jaw and onto her neck. She smelled like apricots. He loved apricots.

Still a bad idea.

His tongue ran along the pulse that fluttered in her neck. And she leaned her head to the side to give him more room.

On second thought, maybe this isn't such a bad idea after all.

She whimpered, and he kissed his way to her lips, his tongue sneaking into her mouth and tangling with hers. She was tentative at first, until he wrapped his arms around her and pulled her closer. She fit perfectly into his arms, and she ran her hands around his back and skimmed them down to grab his ass.

This is the best idea ever.

He pulled back from her and stared into her blown pupils. "Are you sure?"

"Was I not the one who suggested it?"

"What about the food?" He wasn't hungry, but he also didn't want to burn the house down. It would make his father more than a little upset.

"The oven is off. The food is inside it to stay warm. If not, we can heat it up with that magic box in the kitchen later."

He grinned. "The microwave?"

"Yes, that. Can we stop talking now and go back to kissing?"

"Yes, ma'am."

He picked her up in his arms and headed toward the door leading to the hall.

"Wait."

Oh, Fates, had she changed her mind?

"We need the bag on the table."

He snatched the small bag without putting her down and carried her to the guest bedroom. His mouth found hers again for a few moments before setting her down in the middle of the bed.

He handed her the bag, and she pulled out a box of condoms. "Sabrina says we need to be careful after Naya's surprise pregnancy."

"Right."

He pulled off his shirt and toed off his shoes before kneeling on the foot of the bed and gazing at the beauty laid out in front of him. Such fabulous lines, he itched to take her picture. Sergei crawled over her and kissed her nose. Lela scrunched it and then giggled.

"That tickles."

"Good to know. Let's see what else tickles."

He ran his thumb under the strap of her dress and pushed it down her shoulder. "Your skin is like silk."

"Is that a good thing?"

He trailed his fingers across her collarbone. "It's a very good thing." His mouth followed his fingers' path, and he kissed her lightly. His lips made their way up, and he brushed them against her neck. There was something so sexy about her neck.

She angled her head the way she had earlier, as if she was offering herself to him, and he moaned. Damn. He could have spent hours worshipping her neck, but after a few more moments of bliss, fingers wrapped around the back of his head and threaded into his hair. Fingers that directed his kisses to her chin and finally her mouth.

Another favorite part of her. Hell, he wasn't sure if there was a part of her that wasn't a favorite of his.

After a few moments, he pulled away to take a breath, and she actually let out a soft growl. He almost lost it.

"I'm not going anywhere, beautiful. I think there are too many clothes between us."

She lifted her arms up, and he pulled the dress over her head and sucked in a breath. No bra and panties...smooth skin everywhere. The rest of his clothes met the growing pile on the floor, and in moments they were skin to skin.

Why in the world did I ever think this was a bad idea?

And he lost himself in her softness and sweetness before he sheathed himself and hovered over her. "I'll go slow."

"Not too slow, Sergei. I'm not a human woman. Kyle was quite miffed when she found out the first time is not painful for demons."

There were too many people in the bedroom with them right now. Enough distractions. He leaned down and took her mouth before taking her. Or was she taking him?

Glory. Wonder. Damnation.

And they found their own rhythm to a song that only the two of them could hear. Heat shot up his spine and he followed her over the edge.

Afterward, they kissed slowly for a few minutes, until he pushed her tangle of hair away from her eyes and rested his hands on either side of her face.

"I'll be right back." He went to the bathroom and returned moments later to find a sated female lying exactly where he left her.

"Are you okay?"

"I don't have the energy to move."

He grinned, his ego coming out to play. Sergei climbed into bed and covered them both with a blanket as he lay next to her.

"That was amazing."

She blushed. "For me as well. A successful plan."

Sergei wrapped a strand of her hair around his fingers. "So you talked to Sabrina about your plan to seduce me?"

"Yes. We made the plan at girls' night."

Sergei rolled over and pinned her to the bed. "Who else was at this girls' night?"

"Sabrina, Naya, Callie, and Kyle."

Holy Fates, he was never going to live this down.

"They helped me."

He bit her chin lightly. "Let's hear it for Girl Power. Do I need to thank them?"

"If you do, you need to thank Irina too. She made the meal."

Sergei groaned. "Grandmother knows?"

"She's the one who came up with the plan."

He tucked his head against her neck and laughed. Should he be mortified? Thankful? A little bit of both?

He turned onto his side and tucked her against him. "I don't think I'm going to have that particular conversation."

Lela smiled before kissing his chest. "I understand." She ran her foot along his calf.

Sergei placed his fingers under her chin and lifted her face. "What are you up to?"

She batted her eyelashes at him. "I think it would be helpful to practice some more."

He flipped onto his back and pulled her over his stomach so she was straddling him.

Her eyes widened.

"There are a lot of ways to practice."

"Teach me more."

He sat up and kissed her as her fingers fluttered down his chest. She was a quick study.

He gazed into her eyes, and his heart actually thumped like a bass drum.

Why did he feel like she was the one teaching him?

CHAPTER 20

Lela settled into Sergei's warmth as she lay in his arms. Touch. What a simple yet powerful gift. She hoped she would never take moments like this for granted.

Sergei kissed her on the head while a contented rumble vibrated from her chest. He chuckled, and the shaking ran along her back.

"You're purring like a cat. I did promise that I would introduce you to a cat, didn't I? Does that sound mean you're happy?"

"Very." She turned slightly so she could see his face. He smiled down at her, and she almost purred again. "Tell me about yourself, Sergei Chesnokov."

"You already know a lot about me."

She ran her fingers along the scruff on his chin. "I know you travel the earth and take pictures. But tell me more about you."

"What would you like to know?"

"Why don't you have the same accent as your father and Misha? Aleksei sounds a little bit like them at certain times, but you don't. And Misha and Aleksei call Irina babushka, but you call her grandmother."

"Our clan is originally from Russia. Misha is twenty years older than I am, and he was born in Russia, but by the time Aleksei and I were born, Father had moved the clan to Europe."

"What was your childhood like?"

Sergei's eyes lost their light.

"Have I said something wrong?"

"No." He glanced away for a moment before looking at her again. "My childhood was...hard. I lost my mother when I was ten. Of course, Grandmother took care of me, as did Aleksei, even though he was only fifteen at the time."

"What of Misha and your father?"

"Misha came to check on us, but he was grown and married at the time. Father folded in on himself when Mother died, burying himself in work until he was able to move the clan here to the States."

Lela rested her head against Sergei's chest. "I know what it's like to lose a mother. The pain diminishes, but it never goes away."

Sergei rubbed his hand along her arm. "Will you tell me about her?"

Lela snuggled into his chest for a moment to soak up strength. "My mother was killed protecting me."

He placed his fingers under her chin and lifted her face. She looked up into his sad eyes.

"I'm so sorry. You don't have to tell me about it if you don't want to."

"No. That's okay. As you know, over the centuries fewer and fewer females have been born in the realm. When I was born, our clan felt blessed. But the same couldn't be said for the other clans. I am one of the last females to be born in the realm. When I turned seventeen, two Majock demons came for me. They wanted me for themselves, even though we don't know if a Kelmar and Majock demon can even have a child."

Sergei's arms tensed around her, and she placed her hand on his chest.

"My mother fought them and was killed."

"Oh, baby. What happened to the Majock? Did your father wage war on the clan?"

"That was my father's plan. But when the Majock leader found out what his clan members did, he had them put to death. And my father agreed not to wage war."

A small sob erupted from her. "The ironic thing was, I couldn't be the hope of a new generation. I couldn't be touched by anyone, let alone have children."

Sergei kissed her on the forehead. "But now you can be touched."

"Yes."

He pulled her against his chest and she listened to his thudding heartbeat.

"My mother died for me as well. Having me weakened her heart."

Lela's heart ached for him. "And I'm sure she wouldn't have done things differently. Mothers will do anything for their children."

"That's what my father said."

Lela looked up at him. "Then you should listen to him."

He nodded, but she could tell by the look in his eyes that he didn't believe it.

<hr/>

Lela sat at Irina's kitchen counter with a steaming cup of tea, but the chamomile did little to settle her rioting emotions. Sergei had walked her home late last night after they cuddled for a bit and then ate the lasagna Irina helped her make.

Now Lela sat alone in the kitchen waiting for Irina to return from making breakfast for the guards at the community center.

She had been thinking about last night, both the wonder of making love and the discussion they had afterward. Lela wanted to help Sergei, but she wasn't sure exactly how. What she did know was that Irina was the center of this family, and so she would begin with her.

A few minutes later, Irina bustled through the back door grinning.

"Good morning, dear."

"Morning."

"Would you like me to make you something for breakfast?"

"No. I'm not hungry."

Irina's smile dimmed. "Is something wrong? Did last night go poorly? Since you didn't come in until late, I figured the plan worked."

Lela's face heated. "That part went fine."

"Excellent. So what's the problem?"

"Sergei told me about his childhood."

Irina sat down next to her at the counter. "You mean about his mother."

"Yes. He blames himself for her death."

Irina nodded. "Boris and I only learned this recently. Anna's heart weakened after Sergei's birth. Unfortunately, Sergei overheard the doctor tell Boris that he thought it was due to her pregnancy with Sergei. I can't imagine what went through his mind at the time. He was only ten years old, and has been blaming himself ever since. If I could go back in time and strangle that asinine doctor, I would."

Lela grasped Irina's hand. "I told him his mother wanted him."

"Of course she did. Anna was a wonderful wife and mother. She would have done anything for Boris and the boys. But Sergei has let this fester for more than two centuries, and he's made it worse by not feeling worthy."

Lela frowned. "Why would he not..." And then it hit her. "His lack of powers."

"Yes."

"But that's silly."

"You and I know that, but males often feel like they have to prove their worth."

"So how do we help him?"

"By letting him know that, powers or not, he's important to us."

Sergei was definitely important to Lela. She simply needed to find a way to help him understand he was a worthy male.

———◆◇◆———

Lela waited in the examination room of the infirmary for Sabrina to finish typing on the computer. She still didn't fully understand what a computer did, although in this instance she understood that Sabrina was using it to make notes about her patients. Sabrina had asked her to go outside the compound with her for dinner.

Sabrina shut down the computer and turned to her.

"I was going to wait until dinner, but my curiosity is getting the better of me. How did your dinner with Sergei go the other night?"

"Good," Lela said.

Sabrina tilted her head and stared. "Is that all you're going to say?"

Heat rushed up Lela's face. "*Very* good."

Sabrina laughed. "I knew it. Kyle and Callie thought it might take a couple of dates to get Sergei to crack, but I had confidence in you."

"Thanks."

Sabrina gave her a long look. "It was also a big step for you. How do you feel about it?"

Lela thought for a moment before responding. "It wasn't that long ago that I couldn't stand for anyone to touch me. Now, not only have I gained control of my powers, but I have been able to embrace intimacy. I'm happy."

Sabrina smiled. "And I'm happy for you. I count you as a friend now, Lela."

Lela reached over and patted her hand. "As do I. Thank you for being my mentor before I came to earth. If it hadn't been for your wonderful advice, I don't know if I would've come up with the ideas to help with the immigration."

"I was more than happy to help. But I think you would've figured out ways to help without me. I understand you had a good meeting with the Council the other day."

"Hopefully they will embrace the plans we're putting in place."

"You are becoming quite famous," Sabrina said.

"Because of the meeting?"

"Partly. Rumors have been flying around the compound about your ability to heal."

"I pushed my energy into Luke's ankle. I don't think that makes me a healer."

"I agree. But we don't fully know what your power can do, and I want you to be careful."

Nerves danced along Lela's spine. This was actually what she wanted to discuss with her. "I will. Do you think we should find out what I'm capable of?"

Sabrina held up her hand. "Maybe. But I don't want to cause you any stress or injury.

"Agreed."

"We know you were able to reduce Luke's swelling, but his injury wasn't a major trauma. Let's try something simple."

Sabrina picked up a thin silver knife from the metal tray and peeled the clear wrapping from it. She placed the knife against her forearm and made a small cut.

"What are you doing?" Lela gasped.

"I want to see if you can heal torn skin. The cut is small, and my demon metabolism will heal it in a day or two if you can't heal it yourself."

Lela gazed at Sabrina's arm and looked inside. Energy bumped against her skin, trying to escape, much like the blood that welled and ran down the thin cut. Lela concentrated and pushed her energy toward the cut. After a minute she stopped.

"I felt some warmth, but it didn't knit the skin together again. It could be that your powers are more geared toward stressors in the body."

"When I looked at Luke's ankle, the energy swirled around his leg, but it wasn't flowing the right way. I helped unblock it."

"Interesting." Sabrina cleaned her arm before placing a bandage over the cut. "I wonder what ailments would mean a blocking of energy. Sprains, obviously, but it could be other things as well. We obviously can't replicate ailments in a test environment."

"No. But I could work with you like I did in the realm."

Sabrina frowned slightly. "I'm worried that if we expose you in that way, it might put you at risk. I don't want others to take advantage of you. You've already had enough of people stealing your energy."

"But this is different, Sabrina. Now I'm in charge of who I give my energy to. I really want to help."

Sabrina sat down on the stool and rolled it in front of Lela. "Is there someone in particular you're concerned about?"

Why wasn't she surprised that Sabrina had sensed something? "I have been looking inside the demons in the compound. Studying them, actually."

"And what have you found?"

"That energy is the crux of everything. It affects our health, our mood, even our powers. You're right. I do want to try to help someone."

"Who?" Sabrina asked, although Lela was pretty sure she already knew the answer.

"Sergei."

After her night with Sergei and her discussion with Irina, Lela had gone over things again and again in her head. While their childhood stories were shockingly similar, unlike her, Sergei did not feel that his mother's sacrifice had been worthwhile. Lela wanted to grab him and shake him until he got rid of those silly ideas, but she knew it wasn't the true way to help him.

Instead she had looked inside him, and what she found surprised her.

It was time to see if Sergei could find his worth. And if she could help him realize it, all the better.

CHAPTER 21

Sergei headed down the hall of the infirmary. Lela asked him to meet her here, and panic was setting in. Had something happened to her? Had she been attacked again?

He picked up his pace until he found the room number she gave him and opened the door. Lela and Sabrina were sitting calmly in the exam room. It couldn't be that much of a crisis if Sabrina was sitting, right?

Lela smiled at him and patted the seat next to her.

"Is something wrong? Are you okay?" he blurted before he took a seat.

Her eyes widened at his tone. "I'm fine. I'm sorry if I made you worry. I want to discuss something with you."

He looked over at Sabrina, who was wearing a poker face.

"Okay. What do you want to talk about?"

"My powers, and something I've discovered."

He nodded for her to continue.

"You know that I can see the energy inside demons. Now I've been around humans, I've looked inside them as well and discovered their energy is muted. In demons, I see a life force like I see in humans, but I also sense their powers as well. The powers are like a sentient being living inside our skin. I've looked inside you as well."

He frowned. "What are you saying?"

"I'm saying that you don't feel to me like someone without powers. You have energy swirling throughout your body, but it is blocked at the base of your brain, as if a dam has been built there."

"And?"

"And I want to try to help you release it, if you're willing."

He blinked at her. Did he hear her right? "Like you did with Luke?"

"Yes. I don't know if it will do anything for you, but I do know your energy is not in sync with your body. Will you let me try?"

Would he let her try? Hell, yes. "Yes."

Sabrina cleared her throat. "Before we try this, I want to make sure you don't have anything going on with your health. Let's do some neurological exams to make sure the blocked energy is related to your powers."

Sergei nodded. "Fine. Let's do whatever it takes."

"Today's Friday. Let's run some tests now, and we should have the results by Monday. That will give you some time to think about whether you want to try this or not."

"I want to try it."

"Fine. Then we'll go over your results on Monday and go from there. Your father is coming home today, right? And then the celebration dinner is tomorrow night. Have a good weekend, and then we'll figure out next steps."

———————◆O◆———————

Sergei watched Lela and his grandmother walk across the lawn, chatting, on their way to the long table piled high for the outdoor celebration dinner. Luckily it was a warm September evening, and his father had decided to host the festivities outside.

Lela's eyes were wider than normal as she took in the people around her. She still was nervous around large crowds, but his grandmother stayed right by her side. Lela smiled at him as he joined them.

"I'm glad you decided to come tonight."

She shrugged. "Irina didn't give me much choice."

"Well, for once I'm glad her bossiness worked."

"I'm standing right next to you, Sergei. My hearing is just fine."

"I know, Grandmother."

She looked past his shoulder and chuckled. "Here come the twins in full-tilt mode."

Sergei turned in time to squat down and catch both boys as they launched themselves into his arms. "Sergei!"

"Whoa!"

The boys giggled when he tickled them.

When he heard Lela's tinkling laugh, he glanced over to see her whole face light up

Callie rushed across the yard with a frown. "Boys! You need to be careful with all the people around. You have to promise to behave tonight for Miss Irina."

"Yes, Momma," the boys chorused.

"Are you sure it's okay to leave the boys with you tonight?"

"Absolutely. Lela and I have set up sleeping bags for the boys in the living room. After dinner, we're going to watch some cartoons, and then I'm going to tell them some bed-time stories."

Callie hesitated, then squared her shoulders. "Come on, boys. Let's find Misha, and we'll pick out a place to sit together for dinner."

Luke and then Matty raced off to find Misha, with Callie trailing behind them.

Sergei blew out a breath. "Are you sure you two are going to be up to taking care of those two tonight?"

Irina rolled her eyes. "Sergei, I've taken care of you and your brothers and countless other children over the centuries. I can handle it."

He turned to Lela. "What about you?"

"They're delightful. There are very few children left in the realm, so it will be fun to spend time with them."

"How did you get roped into this?"

"Between the immigration and the twins, Callie and Misha don't get to spend time alone together. Callie wants to surprise Misha with a night all to themselves."

Sergei chuckled. "Another seduction plan. It couldn't have happened to a better male."

His grandmother laughed as well. "Wait until you see what your other brother is up to."

He looked over his shoulder. Aleksei was carrying Naya across the lawn. Even several feet away, Sergei could tell Naya was fussing about being carried.

Irina tsked. "I better go save Aleksei from Naya, or maybe Naya from Aleksei. Can you two keep each other company?"

"Of course," Sergei said.

As Irina hurried away, Sergei leaned down and spoke softly in Lela's ear. "Are you overwhelmed yet?"

"I'm fine. It looks like your brothers are both going to have a good evening."

"I've never seen my brothers happier." Which made him happy as well.

Boris called out to the group for everyone to take their seats at the long table. Once everyone was seated, he held up his glass and addressed the guests. "Thank you for all your hard work in making the latest immigration a success."

Sergei clinked his water glass against Lela's, and took a sip before putting it down.

Boris urged everyone to start eating.

Irina had stayed next to Naya and Aleksei at the end of the table. Kyle sat next to a human male and the rest of the BSR team and across from them sat Callie and Misha with the twins.

Just as Misha reached with a serving spoon to fill his plate, Callie whispered something in his ear. The serving spoon landed on his plate with a clatter.

Everyone turned toward them.

"Is everything okay, Mikhail?" Irina asked.

"Yes. Um... I'm not really very hungry."

Silence.

Misha's face turned bright red.

"If you keep losing your appetite, you might want to have the doctor check you over, brother," Aleksei said from his place at the end of the table.

"I think we're going to c-call it a n-night," Misha managed to say.

"Of course, dear. It's been a long day for everyone," Irina said.

Misha stood and pulled out Callie's chair.

"Aren't you going to stay for dessert?" Luke asked.

"I've got some dessert at the house," Callie said, while Kyle choked on a sip of water.

"You boys be good for Miss Irina tonight," Callie said.

"Yes, Momma," they chorused, while Misha practically dragged her around the house and out of sight.

Sergei leaned over and spoke softly in Lela's ear. "My brother seemed unusually eager to leave the party."

Lela chuckled and looked up at him, her eyes sparkling.

The chatter started up again as people settled into the meal, until Aleksei dropped a serving spoon at his end of the table.

"The baby is a she?" he exclaimed as he grabbed Naya's hands.

"Yes. We're having a girl. I was going to tell you later." Naya glanced around at all the gaping faces before sighing. "In private."

Sergei let out a whoop, and Lela applauded along with everyone else. Aleksei stood, scooped Naya into his arms, and carried her away from the table and across the yard.

A few feet before they disappeared around the corner, his brother paused and kissed Naya before striding purposefully away from the dinner.

Everyone else sat in silence for a few moments.

"Are you going to fling silverware across the table like your brothers, Sergei?" Kyle asked.

Sergei grinned. "Nope."

Irina picked up her fork. "I don't know about the rest of you, but I'm not going to let this good food go to waste."

Sergei winked at Lela before digging in. His brothers were happy, and he was happy for them. And if all went well on Monday, he might have his own good news to share.

CHAPTER 22

Sabrina set down the computer tablet and looked at Sergei. "All the tests came back negative. There's nothing physically wrong with you that I can find."

Sergei blew out the breath he had been holding. "That's a good thing."

"Yes," Sabrina said. She held up her hands in front of his face and closed her eyes for a moment.

Sergei looked across the room at Lela, who was standing next to the door. She smiled at him, and his nerves settled down a bit.

Sabrina lowered her hands. "I still sense the blockage that Lela can see. Have you decided to let her try to get it moving?"

"Yes."

"I think it's best if you lie on the gurney on your stomach, and then we'll have Lela work on you."

Sergei climbed up and lay down, turning his head to face Lela. She walked over to him and rested her hands lightly on his back.

"Are you ready?"

"Yes."

Lela ran her hands up his spine to the base of his skull. Warmth spread from her fingertips and up into his head, and Sergei sighed.

"Are you okay?" Lela asked.

"Yes."

She continued to run her fingers around his neck, and the warmth increased until he was almost lulled to sleep. He wasn't sure how much time had passed until she lifted her fingers from his skin, and he wanted to ask her to touch him again.

"How do you feel?" Lela asked.

"Okay."

"Sit up slowly," Sabrina advised.

Sergei sat while Sabrina examined him, first with a stethoscope, and then she shined a penlight in his eyes. She nodded before raising her hands and circling him slowly.

"I definitely feel your energy moving around freely. I don't know what was blocking you, but it seems to be gone now." She stopped in front of him again. "Do you feel different? Any surges of energy?"

"I feel relaxed, but otherwise nothing has changed." He tried to hide his disappointment. He didn't know what he'd expected, exactly. It wasn't like he would all of a sudden be able to leap tall buildings or run faster than a locomotive.

Sabrina gave him a small smile. "We've never tried something like this before. If Lela did release your powers, I don't know that the change would be immediately evident. I want you to come again to see me tomorrow. We'll see how you're doing then."

He nodded as his phone buzzed in his pocket, and frowned when he looked at the screen. "It's from Misha. He wants me to come to Callie's tonight for a meeting."

Sabrina's phone beeped as well. "Same with me. I wonder what's going on?"

Their phones chimed again. "It's Misha again," Sergei said. "Says it's not bad news, but we should show up or he will hunt us down."

Sabrina shook her head. "I love your brother, even if he is a bit over the top." She tucked her phone back into her pocket. "You still feeling okay?"

"Yes."

"What does his energy look like now, Lela?"

"It's flowing around his body and up into his head."

"Okay. After you go to Misha's meeting, Sergei, I want you to take it easy tonight, and then we'll check you again tomorrow."

Sergei stood and straightened his shirt. "I'll be here same time tomorrow."

Lela followed him out into the infirmary hall.

"Are you truly okay?" she asked.

"Of course. I knew this was a long shot. At the very least, you got my energy moving again. Even though Sabrina didn't find anything wrong with me, I can't imagine the blockage was healthy."

She reached for him, and he wrapped his hand around hers as they continued down the hall. He didn't know which one of them was more disappointed. And a small part of him wondered if part of Lela's disappointment was because he was still powerless.

Sergei rounded the back of Callie's house and found a large group already gathered in the backyard. Misha's BSR team was there—Kyle, Jean Luc, Talia, and Jason. Irina had mentioned that Kyle had a mate by the name of Dalton, and Sergei decided the human male who was with Kyle at dinner Saturday night and now had his arm draped around her must be Dalton.

Sabrina was on the patio chatting with Irina and Lela, and Boris was watching the boys horse around on their playset. When someone called to him from behind, Sergei turned to see Naya hustling toward him and Aleksei following a few feet behind her.

Naya reached for Sergei and wrapped her arm around his. "I jumped out of the car before he had it in park. Lead me around back before your brother tries to carry me again."

Sergei laughed. "Yes, ma'am."

He led Naya over to a patio chair, and she sat down.

Aleksei shot him a glare before he came to stand behind Naya.

Everyone seemed to be accounted for...except Misha and Callie. Sergei caught bits and pieces of conversation. His grandmother seemed to be in peak form today.

"I was watching a show on TV today featuring an interview with a bunch of twentysomethings." Irina rolled her eyes. "Millennials think they have it so hard. They should try being a millennium and see how they like it."

Lela was trying very hard not to laugh, but Sabrina didn't do so well, giggling, and then laughing till tears streamed down her face.

"You're right, Irina."

The French doors opened, Misha and Callie walked out onto the patio, and the group quieted down.

Misha beamed at everyone. "Thanks for coming tonight. We would like to tell you all something." He smiled down at Callie and nodded.

"Misha asked me to marry him Saturday night."

The group erupted into cheers and applause. Hugs and backslaps ensued, and then everyone settled down to hear the story.

"Way to go, Mish!" Kyle said. "You sly devil. You didn't tell any of us you were going to propose."

Misha smiled. "It was the right time, and I didn't want an audience."

"But it's Monday. Why didn't you tell us sooner?" Irina asked.

"I had to ask the boys' permission to marry their mother first."

Kyle blinked several times. "Dang it, Mish. I'm going to cry."

Misha's grin widened. "The boys asked me if they could call me papa."

"I can't stop them now," Kyle said as a couple tears ran down her cheek. "You're a dad now, Mish."

Misha cleared his throat. "I know."

The boys ran over to the group. "Did you hear?" Luke blurted breathlessly. "We're getting a papa."

Matty darted over to Boris. "Are you our grandpa now?"

Boris knelt down in his Armani suit, apparently grass stains be damned, and hugged the boys to him. Boris turned them around so they faced the crowd.

"Yes, I'm your grandpa. You also have uncles and aunts now, too. And a great-grandmother."

Aleksei placed his hand on Naya's stomach. "And a cousin coming soon, too."

"Someone get me a box of tissues." Kyle said soggily as the tears continued to trickle down her cheeks.

Boris handed her a handkerchief, and she wiped her eyes.

"We have champagne chilling. Let me go grab the bottles," Callie said.

"We'll get them," Sabrina and Talia volunteered.

"Have you decided on a date yet?" Irina asked as the champagne was poured.

"We've been talking about what we want, but not the date yet," Misha said. "I was thinking October."

Callie's mouth dropped open. "Misha, that's less than a month away."

"I don't want to wait a year to marry you, Callie."

"What about Naya?" Callie turned to her. "When are you due?"

"The baby is scheduled to come toward the end of October."

Misha wrapped his arm around Callie's shoulder. "Then we have the wedding the second weekend of the month, before the baby arrives. What do you think?"

Callie's eyes sparkled as she gazed up at Misha. "Let's do it."

Irina rubbed her hands together. "I'll help Callie with the arrangements. Since it's short notice, would you like to have the ceremony here in the compound? The beginning of October is usually warm. We could even plan something out by the lake, and then have the reception catered and served in the community center."

Misha's eyes lit up. "Food. I have some ideas about that."

Callie laughed. "Somehow I knew you would."

Misha cleared his throat. "Jean Luc, you will be my best man, or best vampire, yes?"

The vampire smiled, his fangs peeking out. "I would be honored."

"And Aleksei and Sergei will be groomsmen."

Aleksei chuckled. "I don't know, Sergei. Did he just ask us, or order us?"

Sergei crossed his arms and mock-glared at Misha. "I think that was an order."

"Don't make me dangle you guys in the air until you agree," Misha said.

Sergei couldn't hold his angry face any longer, and laughed along with Aleksei.

Callie chimed in. "I'm going to ask my friend Jill to be my matron of honor, because we wouldn't be here without her. She's the one who called the BSR the first time the twins showed their powers in public."

"I made a fireball at soccer practice," Matty announced.

"It's not something I'll forget anytime soon, sweetie. Kyle, will you be my maid of honor?"

Kyle's mouth opened and then closed again. Sergei had never seen her so flustered before. "Um, I'm honored, Callie, but I don't know anything about being a maid of honor. I'd be better off as a groomswoman."

Misha chuckled. "Little one—"

"What if I officiate the wedding?" Kyle interrupted him. "I could marry you both. The internet makes it easy now. If I can convince the Demon Council to allow the realm demons to come to earth, I can stand in front of wedding guests and marry you two, right?"

"Actually, Callie and I have been talking Father, we would like you to marry us," Misha said.

Boris blinked several times, and Kyle pressed his water-logged handkerchief against his chest.

"I would be honored, son."

"So that means maid of honor for you, little one. And you can be the backup for Father in case he can't perform the ceremony for any reason."

"I'm not going to need to watch my back, am I, Kyle?"

"Ha, ha. Very funny." Kyle shuddered. "Dresses, flowers, wedding showers, all those things are foreign to me."

"Talia and I will help," Sabrina said. "Lela can help too."

"What do we get to do?" Luke asked.

"I don't want to carry a pillow," Matty said.

"We have a special job for both of you," Misha said, squatting down in front of them. "Much more important than being ring bearers."

"What?" they blurted together.

"Your momma would like you to walk her down the aisle. Would you like to do that?"

"Yes!" They chimed in together and ran over to Callie and each grabbed a hand. "We need to practice."

"Damn. Here I go again," Kyle sniffled. "Boris, I need your handkerchief back."

Boris replied in a soggy voice, "Can't. It's being used."

Sergei's eyes blurred too. He searched out Lela's face. She had tears in her eyes as well. It was amazing how quickly she was fitting into his wild family. Amazing and a little scary.

Everyone started throwing out ideas to the bride and groom, and Sergei sat down in an empty chair to watch his family.

A slight buzzing sounded in his head, and he blinked as the sensation intensified. Champagne could go to your head, but he only had a sip. He set the glass down and blinked.

Pain shot behind his eyes, down into his neck, and the buzz turned into voices, dozens of voices, all talking inside his head. He couldn't understand, and they started to get louder.

Sergei slapped his hands over his ears. Why was everyone screaming at him?

Aleksei reached for him, and he jerked away. Aleksei's mouth was moving, as were his other family members' mouths, as they gathered around him, but he couldn't make out what everyone were saying, since their voices were also slamming around inside his head.

What's wrong?

He looks like he's about to pass out.

Is he sick?

Sergei!

He pushed his chair back hard, and it tipped over, crashing on the patio. He scrambled away from them, flattening himself against the back of the house. Panic wrapped around his spinal cord like choking tendrils, and the voices pressed in to smother him. He had to get away.

Misha and Aleksei stood in front of him with their hands raised. But he didn't want them near him. He needed them to all shut up. He slid his back along the wall to make a break for it, but an invisible force stopped him.

He pushed against the force, but he couldn't move.

"Let me go!" he screamed at Misha.

Sergei searched for Lela, and stared into her panicked eyes right before the voices pushed him into the darkness.

CHAPTER 23

Lela hovered in the corner of the waiting room with Sergei's worried family and friends. The same family and friends who were celebrating less than an hour ago.

Even when Tarem attacked her in the realm, she hadn't been as scared as she was right now. What was wrong with Sergei? Had she caused it?

Misha and Aleksei paced the room while everyone else sat in the chairs lining the walls.

"What the hell happened?" Aleksei asked for the hundredth time as he paced by Misha.

"Sabrina will let us know as soon as she can," Irina said.

Lela couldn't stand there and not say anything. Not if this was her fault.

She cleared her throat. "I might know what caused this."

All eyes turned to her, and she faltered for a moment. But she wasn't going to back down now. They all had the right to know.

"What do you mean?" Irina asked.

"Sabrina and I have been working with Sergei. I noticed that he had a blockage at the base of his skull that stopped energy from traveling into his head. Sabrina ran tests, and when she didn't find anything wrong with his health, I tried to unblock the energy."

"Like you did with Luke?" Misha asked.

"Yes."

"Did it work?" Kyle asked.

Lela nodded. "Yes, both Sabrina and I could sense that his energy flow was normal after I worked on him, and we hoped that it might mean that he actually does have powers."

"Why didn't he say anything?" Boris asked.

"He didn't want to get anyone's hopes up."

Aleksei let out a hard breath. "When is he going to realize that we don't care if he has powers or not? *Damn* it!"

Lela flinched. "I'm sorry."

Aleksei's eyes widened. "That wasn't directed at you, Lela. It's just that I'm worried."

So was she. She could barely draw air into her lungs.

A few moments later Sabrina joined them.

"Is Sergei all right?" multiple voices asked.

"He's fine right now. I gave him a light sedative to get him to relax."

Boris stood. "What happened to him?"

"His brain is on overload right now. He's hearing every-one's thoughts."

"He's telepathic now?" Aleksei asked.

"Yes. From what I can tell, he's a telepath whose powers have been blocked for centuries and suddenly switched on. The problem is, all the stimuli are crowding into his brain at once."

"So he must be overloading," Irina said.

Naya frowned. "If he's hearing thoughts without permission, his telepathic abilities are extremely strong. I can carry on telepathic conversations with people who are willing, but I can't pull thoughts from them."

"So how do we help him?" Kyle asked.

"We first need to help him get a handle on his powers. I'm worried he'll retreat into himself if he can't control them."

"I can help," Naya said.

"And I'm going to take you up on that, but tonight I want to get him calmed down," Sabrina said. "I know you all want to see him, but he can't handle the stimulus."

"Okay. But we want to do something," Misha said.

"And you can. First, I'm going to check on Sergei again, and then we'll discuss next steps. He did ask to see Lela, if you're up to it?"

Lela's lungs rebelled, trying to block her ability to breathe. Did he blame her for what happened? Would he be able to forgive her?

She nodded and followed Sabrina down the hall. After a few steps, Sabrina stopped and placed her palms on Lela's shoulders. "Before we go into his room, you need to push your thoughts away like you do your energy. Block them so Sergei can't hear them."

Lela frowned.

"You can do it. Take those thoughts and build a wall around them."

Lela closed her eyes and built the mental wall, then took her fears and thoughts and locked them in a room in her mind with a large metal door, hidden behind the wall.

After a minute she opened her eyes and nodded.

"Excellent. Are you ready?"

"Yes."

Sabrina opened the door and they entered Sergei's hospital room. He tensed when they walked in, then looked between them, and after a few seconds he relaxed.

"It's quiet. I can't hear you."

Sabrina stepped up to the bed. "We're both suppressing our thoughts right now."

Lela held herself back by the door so she wouldn't overwhelm him.

"Tell me what's happening to me," Sergei said.

"We think when Lela helped unblock your energy, she jumpstarted your powers. You're a telepath."

Sergei shook his head. "I'm confused. I know several telepaths in our clan. They can talk to others through their minds. Naya is one of them. But they don't hear thoughts without permission."

"No. But I have met a few select telepaths who could hear thoughts without being invited. Very powerful telepaths."

Sergei rubbed the back of his neck. "I find it ironic that my entire life I've wanted powers, and now I have them, I can't live with them."

"I'm sorry," Lela said.

"You have nothing to be sorry about. I hoped you could help me be a better demon."

"You're already a good demon, Sergei."

"How do I stop the voices?" he asked Sabrina.

"You learn to control it. If this had come on gradually as a child, you would have more than likely learned to block the voices as part of your normal progression. Instead, the floodgates burst open all at once, and you don't have the skills to manage them."

"Like me," Lela said.

"Like you. Which means we teach Sergei to block the voices."

"Yes," Lela said, nodding with conviction.

Lela reached for him, and he flinched, causing her to step back.

"I'm sorry," he said.

"No, I'm sorry. Of all people, I should know better than to reach for someone like that. You're in pain right now."

Sabrina looked between the two of them. "I'm going to spend a few minutes helping you try to block the voices. Then we're going to get you settled for the night."

"Then what?"

"Lela is going to go spend some time with your family so she can, with Naya's help, show them how to block their thoughts."

Sergei actually smiled slightly. "Good luck with that. They can't keep their opinions to themselves under normal circumstances. How are you going to get them to contain their thoughts?"

"They'll do it. They're very anxious to help," Lela said.

His smile slipped. "That's just my family. You can't teach the world to block me."

Sabrina sat down in the chair next to the bed. "No. But I can teach you how to block everyone. Naya has volunteered to help as well."

"Which means Aleksei won't be too far away."

Sabrina nodded. "More than likely. Now let's get to work."

Lela left the room and hurried down the hall to the sea of anxious faces.

"How is he?" Boris asked.

"Good. He's still got his sense of humor. Sabrina is spending time with him working on blocking the voices. In the meantime, with Naya's help, if she is willing, I'm going to teach you how to block your thoughts so you can be around Sergei."

Irina nodded. "Yes. Please teach us. I want to be able to see my grandson tomorrow."

Lela sat down and started to explain, and the normally rambunctious group quieted down and paid close attention to her and Naya's instructions.

Everything had to be okay. Lela couldn't accept any other outcome.

The next morning Lela was at the hospital early. She couldn't help herself. She had to know how Sergei was doing.

Sabrina met her in the hall.

"What time did you get here?" Lela asked.

"I actually never left. I slept in the doctors' lounge so I'd be close by if Sergei needed anything."

"How did he do overnight?"

"Not too bad. I worked with him for a little bit, and he started to get the hang of things, but when he tried to go to bed, he would relax and then he would hear the thoughts of the night staff. I gave him another sedative to help him sleep."

"Naya and I worked with the family last night as well. They're all trying very hard to suppress their thoughts so they can visit Sergei."

"I'm surprised they aren't standing in line behind you."

Lela smiled. "Sergei is lucky to have such loving family and friends."

"Yes, he is."

"Can I go spend some time with him?"

"Of course. Remember to block before you enter the room."

Lela went to Sergei's room and knocked.

"Come in."

Opening the door, Lela found Sergei sitting in a chair by the window.

"You're up."

"Yes. I'm more than capable of getting out of bed."

"I'm sorry. I didn't mean anything."

Sergei stood. "No. I'm sorry. I don't mean to snap at you." He stared at her for a moment. "You're doing a good job of blocking your thoughts from me."

"It's similar to what I do when I block my energy."

"I have heard some interesting thoughts. Apparently, the night nurse and the orderly like each other but they're scared to say anything."

"Are you thinking about playing matchmaker?"

"Where did you learn that word? Wait, never mind. You're living with my grandmother."

Lela laughed. "Yes, she has told me her mission in life is to find matches for everyone in the clan."

"Why am I not surprised?"

"When I saw Sabrina in the hall, she said you did well with your lessons last night."

Sergei grimaced slightly. "I can keep the voices away if I concentrate, but I can't do it all the time."

"I felt the same way when Sabrina trained me. It will become second nature soon, I think." She looked down at the floor. "I want to apologize again."

"No. Stop."

"I can't. I shouldn't have pushed you to try this."

"Lela. You didn't push me. I wanted to do it. The bottom line is that I have powers now, something I never thought I would have, so I can't complain. I would have liked not to feel like someone tried to drive a spike in my brain last night, but I'm not going to complain. Got it?"

"Yes."

Sergei walked over to the window. "How's my family doing?"

"They're all very worried about you. Aleksei, especially, was extremely upset last night."

Sergei turned back to her. "He's always been overprotective of me since our mother died."

"You told me he took care of you."

"Yes. Even though he was only fifteen at the time and he'd lost his mother too. As I got older, I pushed him away."

"Which most children do with their parents. You were trying to find your own path."

"Right. You are a ridiculously smart female."

Lela shrugged. "You say that like you're surprised."

"Not surprised. More in awe."

Heat rushed up Lela's cheeks.

"I love when you blush. Such a pretty shade of pink."

More heat flooded her face. She was probably as red as the apple Irina gave her yesterday.

A light knock on the door saved her from more embarrassment.

Aleksei and Misha stood in the doorway.

"Are you up to visitors?" Misha asked.

"Yes."

Lela beckoned them into the room. "Come in. I'll let you three talk."

"We don't want to chase you off," Aleksei said.

"You're not. I'll return later. I promised to help your grandmother with breakfast this morning."

"Babushka is a taskmaster," Misha said. "She'll come hunting you down if you don't show up."

Lela nodded before turning to Sergei. "I'll be back later if you'd like me to visit again."

"Definitely."

She left the brothers to their visit, her heart settling into its normal rhythm now she knew he was doing better.

Lela would not be able to live with herself if she hurt him.

Sergei watched Lela leave the room, and he had to stop himself from calling her back. When had she become the meaning of calm to him?

"How are you doing?" Misha asked.

"Better." He cleared his throat. "I'm sorry I ruined your announcement."

Misha sighed. "Don't be ridiculous. You didn't ruin anything. Callie and I are still getting married. And you're not getting out of being a groomsman."

Sergei nodded and looked over at Aleksei, who hovered a few feet away. His brother had deep furrows across his forehead.

"Wow, Aleksei. Chill out. I'm fine."

"Are you really?"

"I will be. I'm already better than last night."

"How did it feel last night?" Aleksei asked.

"Like a million voices screaming in my head. Today it's much more controlled." Sergei laughed. "Holy Fates, Misha. Are you singing "You Are My Sunshine" in your head?"

Misha blanched. "Yes. Sorry. I've been working on blocking my thoughts like Lela explained last night, and I've been having trouble, so I concentrate on something else."

"I don't need to hear your thoughts to know you're both worried about me. I get it. But I also know I have finally been given powers. Something I never thought to have in this life."

Aleksei shook his head. "They're not worth you being hurt."

"I think I should be the judge of that."

"Should you? Because I don't think you can be objective. You are so hell-bent on proving yourself that you forget we don't care whether you have powers or not."

"Aleksei," Misha's voice lowered.

"I'm not sorry for wanting to keep Sergei safe."

Sergei held up his hand. "It's okay, Misha." He turned to face Aleksei. "Thank you."

Where's the but? Aleksei thought.

There is no but. Sergei replied telepathically.

Aleksei jerked back, face pale.

"What's going on?" Misha barked.

"Sorry, Misha. It was rude to leave you out of the conversation. I responded to Aleksei telephathically. But I'll say the rest out loud so you can hear too. When Mother died, Aleksei, you took care of me even though you were in pain too. I can never begin to repay you for that."

Pain seared into Sergei's thoughts from both his brothers.

"Don't feel guilty, Misha. You were there for us as well. You were dealing with the arranged marriage Father insisted on while he was dealing with his own emotions. Thank you both. The fact that you don't care whether or not I have powers tells me how lucky I am to have you as brothers."

Sergei backed away from his brothers, who were both projecting their turbulent emotions quite loudly.

"How can we help you?" Aleksei asked.

"You're doing it by being here for me when I need it. Right now, I'm starting to get a headache from all this brotherly concern and love. Do you mind if I boot you out so I can relax for a bit?"

"Of course not," Misha said. "Why don't we call you later? I don't think you should be able to hear our thoughts over the phone. We can do that for a day or two until we all get a handle on this."

Sergei nodded. "Sounds like a plan." He backed up another step so they couldn't hug him. He didn't think he could handle the contact right now.

Misha opened the door and they both left, leaving him in quiet, but not in peace. Their emotions still saturated the air, and he had a hard time sucking a clean breath into his lungs.

Everything was going to be all right. He would not finally be given these powers only to be unable to control them. The Fates weren't that cruel...were they?

CHAPTER 24

His brain went quiet.

He had been working so hard to contain the noise, but wayward thoughts popped up at the most inopportune times. He'd felt like a telepathic peeping Tom for the past two days. Not something to be proud of.

When the voices silenced, it jarred Sergei out of a deep sleep. He knew immediately that his powers were gone. Sucked away into the void. He lay in the early morning light, staring at the white squares of the hospital room ceiling, and blew out a breath. Where had they gone? He had worried about not being able to contain them, not about losing them.

Damn. The Fates were evil.

The door opened and he jumped. He hadn't sensed anyone coming.

Sabrina appeared at his bedside, frowning. "What's wrong?"

He pushed back the covers and sat up. "My powers are gone."

"Maybe you've finally mastered blocking the voices."

He shook his head. "No. This is different. I can't hear anything."

She moved closer and held her hands above him, closing her eyes for a minute before opening them again.

"I still sense that your energy is unblocked. It's moving up into your brain."

"Maybe my powers have nothing to do with my energy."

"What do you mean?"

"We're avoiding the obvious answer here. It could be that the powers were never mine. That Lela gave them to me, and now they've worn off."

"Lela isn't telepathic."

"No but she is powerful. More powerful than I think we understand. Is it totally out of the realm of possibility that she somehow did this?"

"I don't want to guess, so I'm not going to answer that until we have more information."

"And how do we do that?"

"Let's call Naya. It makes sense to bring another telepath into the mix. She can sense your telepathic energy."

"Or lack thereof."

"Don't give up yet, Sergei."

He nodded, even though he was feeling far from optimistic. He wanted to believe he had a chance at keeping his powers, but he couldn't shake the feeling that they weren't his to begin with.

Lela found Aleksei pacing in the hall in the infirmary.

"Has something happened?"

"Sabrina asked Naya to come spend some time with Sergei."

"What's wrong?" she asked as her heart pounded in her ears.

"Sergei says he's lost his telepathic ability."

No. Lela pushed past Aleksei and raced down the hall and into Sergei's room. Sergei was sitting on the bed with Naya standing in front of him, her hands resting on either side of his face. Sabrina stood at the foot and held her hand up to stop Lela from going farther into the room.

"I'm sorry, but I don't sense any telepathic energy, Sergei." Naya dropped her hands.

"Thanks for coming. I'm sure Aleksei is pacing out in the hall. You should probably go calm him down."

"He's worried about you."

"Tell him I'm fine."

Naya nodded slightly at Lela before leaving.

"I don't understand what's going on. I can see that Sergei's energy is still moving," Lela said.

"I can sense it too." Sabrina ran her hand along the stethoscope around her neck. Lela had learned that she often did that when she was trying to figure something out.

"So what happened?"

Sergei looked at her. "I think you gave me the powers."

Lela's stomach twisted like it had when she first went through the portal. "I couldn't have."

"Why not? We know you can enhance powers in demons. Who says you can't give powers as well?"

"I'm not a telepath. How could I give you something I don't have?" She turned to Sabrina. "Tell him this is impossible."

"I don't know that I can, Lela. We don't know enough to rule it out."

"So let's put it to the test," Sergei said. "Give me some of your energy, and we'll see if the powers come back."

As much as she didn't want to do this, it was the only way to prove him wrong. Lela placed her hands on his neck and gazed into his beautiful brown eyes. Eyes that were missing their normal spark, as if he'd shuttered his emotions away from her.

She swallowed and pushed a little bit of her energy into him. After a minute she pulled her hands away.

"Do you feel different?" she asked.

"Not yet. But the last time it took a few hours before I felt anything."

Sabrina said, "Why don't you two relax for a bit, then? I've got to finish some paperwork and get the doctors here up to speed on some things."

Sergei frowned at her departure. "What did she mean about getting doctors up to speed?"

"Sabrina actually works for the BSR team. She has been pulling double duty here since she's helping with the immigration."

Sergei got up and walked over to the window. "Double duty. You're sounding more like an earther every day."

Lela shrugged. "This is my home, and I want to learn."

"Of course you do. That's what I admire about you, your willingness to embrace new things."

She went over and stood between him and the window. "We'll figure this out. I don't want you to give up on this." *Please don't hate me.*

"I could never hate you."

Lela had trouble breathing. She hadn't said that last part out loud. She looked up at him to see his eyes filled with resignation.

"Well that solves that."

She blinked to stop the tears. "I didn't do it on purpose."

"I know you didn't."

He held out his hand to her, and she grasped it. A tear spilled down her cheek right before he pulled her against him.

"Don't cry, Lela. You are such a wonderful female. To wish for something so much for me that you gave me powers is incredible."

She nodded against his chest. She wasn't sure how long they stood like that, but when the door opened and Sabrina walked in, Lela took a step back from him.

"Did something happen?"

"My...the powers are back."

Sabrina's eyes narrowed. "Okay. So we'll monitor your powers and see how long they last. Maybe they'll be permanent this time."

"Maybe," Sergei said, although his pinched expression told Lela he didn't believe what he was saying.

He looked down at her, and she didn't have to be telepathic to know he was going to say something she wouldn't like.

"Lela. I think it would make sense for you to go."

"Why?"

"Because we need to see if I can hold the powers on my own."

"I won't share any more energy with you."

"No, but we don't know if I might be draining energy from you without knowing I am. All this is new to me, and I don't know how to control it."

Lela swallowed, then swallowed again. She was not going to cry, especially when she looked at Sabrina's concerned face. She nodded, since her throat hurt and she couldn't think of what to say anyway, and walked toward the door. Why did it feel like they were saying goodbye?

Lela shoved her rioting emotions into the room in her brain with the big metal door and slammed it shut with a thump that vibrated all the way to her heart.

CHAPTER 25

He was back to the same old Sergei again. No powers. The telepathy had only lasted a day this time. He sat on the examination table while Sabrina stood with her hands above his head. After a few moments, she lowered her hands.

"I don't sense any changes to your energy flow. I could call Naya—"

"Don't bother, Sabrina. They're gone."

She took a step back from him and stared at him hard. "How do you feel otherwise?"

"Is that your roundabout way of asking me if I'm depressed?"

"Possibly. I've been trying to think of some tests we could run. Something neurological—"

"Not right now, okay?"

"Sure."

"Will you discharge me? I've been here long enough."

"Of course. I don't see any reason to keep you here. But if you have any problems, you'll call me right?"

"Yes, doctor."

Sabrina scowled. "Don't use your sarcasm on me. You forget I've dealt with both your brothers for a while now, and I've heard it all."

Sergei smiled slightly. "Point taken."

"Lela came to see how you were doing a couple times. I don't understand why you won't let me tell her what's going on."

"Sorry to pull the doctor-patient confidentiality card, but I decided I want to be the one to tell her."

Sabrina studied him for a moment. "I'm going to fill out your discharge papers to get you out of here. I'll be back in a few minutes."

Sergei stood in the room for a few quiet minutes. After the initial overload of voices, it was interesting how quickly his body had gotten used to the constant buzz of thoughts. And when the silence came again, he actually mourned the loss. And that scared him.

But what terrified him even more was the thought, even though it was fleeting, that he could ask Lela to give him the powers again.

Unacceptable.

Sabrina leaned in and said, "You're free to go."

"Thanks."

"Your brothers came to see how you're doing, and they're waiting in the hall to escort you home."

"I don't need their escort."

Sabrina snorted. "Do you honestly think I was going to dissuade them from that? They even discussed using a wheelchair to take you home."

"I'm going to kick both their asses."

"Please don't. I'd prefer not to have to patch any of you up." Sabrina's smile slipped. "Now you're officially discharged, I have something to say—not as your doctor. I'm going to say something you might not want to hear.

"Don't push Lela away. She's already blaming herself for this. She cares about you, Sergei."

He couldn't promise anything. "Thanks for taking care of me, Sabrina."

Her eyes tightened before she nodded and opened the door for him. What Sabrina didn't understand was that Sergei only had Lela's well-being at heart.

He quickly found his brothers standing at the door with twin grins on their faces.

"They're finally letting you out of here," Aleksei said.

Sergei nodded. "Let's go. I need some fresh air."

The three of them walked outside, the fall air chilling Sergei as he took a deep breath. They walked in silence for a minute, which surprised Sergei, since between his two brothers, they never stopped talking.

"Why aren't you talking?" he asked.

"We're trying to give you space," Misha said.

Sergei looked to his brother on his right and then the one on his left. "This is giving me space?"

"Shut up," Aleksei said. "Tell us what happened."

Sergei sighed before quickly explaining.

"So Lela was giving you powers?" Misha summed it up.

"Yes. I never had my own powers. Still a null."

"Stop calling yourself that! There is nothing wrong with you," Aleksei said.

"Easy for you to say, since you can shoot fireballs."

Aleksei got right up in his face. "If I could, I would give you my powers. I don't need them. Damn it, Sergei. Didn't we just go through this with the elder council? Misha is the strongest one of us, but I have been chosen to lead the clan. My powers don't make me a leader. *I* do."

"I know that. And I accepted it until I was given a taste of what it's like to have powers, only to have them yanked away from me."

Aleksei's eyes softened. "And I know that too. It has to suck, and I'm sorry."

Sergei backed away. He couldn't handle a bear hug from his brother right now.

He turned to Misha. A change of subject was in order. "Have you set the date for your wedding?"

Misha grinned. "Potentially. We wanted to make sure you're okay before we finalize the date. It's the second Saturday in October."

"I will definitely be back for that."

"Back?" Aleksei frowned.

"I have a photo shoot I have to complete for a magazine before the end of October. I'm going to go now so I can be back in time for the wedding."

"And the birth?"

Sergei nodded. "And the birth."

"Do you think you should go now, so soon after getting out of the hospital?" Misha asked.

"I'm not sick. I'll be fine."

They both looked like they were going to argue with him. "Don't make me kick your asses."

"I'd like to see you try, little brother," Aleksei growled.

Misha wiggled his eyebrows at him. "What *he* said."

Sergei shook his head and started walking again, his brothers falling in step on either side. He needed to get away for a while to clear his head and, more importantly, his heart.

His brothers escorted him to Boris's house, and his father naturally showed up to hover over him as well. After an hour, Sergei escaped from their overprotective clutches and headed toward his grandmother's house.

He walked around the house and saw Irina through the windows in the kitchen. When he opened the door, he was greeted with a big smile and the scent of warm oatmeal cookies. Another one of his favorites.

"Are these for me?"

"Yes. I was going to bring them to you at the hospital, but this is even better."

Sergei nodded. "I came to tell you what happened. Where's Lela?"

"She's resting right now. Even though she hasn't said anything to me, I know she hasn't been sleeping well."

"Let's not wake her now. I'll talk to her later."

"Why do I feel like I should sit down for this conversation?"

"How much has Lela told you?"

"Pretty much everything she knows. She's been holding her breath, waiting to hear if you still have your powers."

"I don't."

Irina closed her eyes. "I'm sorry, dear. I know how important this is to you. But you can't let it get you down."

"I'm not. But I am going to leave for a bit on a photo assignment." He held up his hand. "Don't worry, I've already been threatened by both Misha and Aleksei if I don't get back here for the wedding and the birth of my niece."

"You do what you need to do, Sergei, to get your head on straight again, but you need to come back home to your family. Don't make me come find you myself."

"No, ma'am."

Lela walked in. "Sergei, you're here."

Something sharp twisted in his stomach at the sound of her anxious voice.

Irina stood and picked up the plate of cookies siting on the counter. "I promised to take some of these to the twins. I'll leave you two alone to talk."

Sergei gestured to the chair Irina had just vacated and Lela sat down, her posture stiff.

"Are you okay?"

"The powers are gone."

She looked down at her hands, which were clenched together on the table.

"I'm okay, Lela. I figured this would be the outcome. I've been thinking through a lot of things this past day, while I was waiting to see when the powers would leave me. I've made some decisions."

She looked up at him. "And what decisions have you made?"

He pushed out a breath. "I'm leaving for a few weeks for a photography job."

She froze. "You're leaving."

"Yes."

"Because of what I did to you?"

"No! It's time for me to start working again. I can't stay here indefinitely." He swallowed. "I just want to make sure I hadn't given you any expectations about us being a long-term thing."

"What does 'long-term thing' even mean?"

Shit. He was screwing this up royally. "We can't be together."

"Why not?"

"I said from the beginning that I was going to leave again."

"Yes, you did," she replied, gazing at him with her soft green eyes.

"This can't work, Lela. The powers you gave me aren't mine. It's too tempting, with you being so close by, to ask for them again."

"But it doesn't hurt me."

"That's not the point. I won't take advantage of you the way the others did. You have only recently learned how to let people touch you. I don't want you ever to think I'm using you for your powers."

"Sergei—"

"No. I want you to be happy and find your place in this world with someone who won't hurt you. I'm not that person."

Lela pushed back the chair and stood. She stared at him until he almost flinched under her scrutiny. Instead he steadied his breathing, even though his heart was rioting in his chest.

"Have you finished making decisions for both of us?" Lela asked.

"Yes."

"So you are leaving your family again."

"For work."

She narrowed her eyes. "You're running away. You tell me all the time how sorry you are that in the past I couldn't let anyone close to me because of my powers. At least in my case, until I learned how to control them, there was a legitimate reason for living in isolation. What's your excuse?"

Sergei lurched back as her words pierced him, but she continued.

"You won't let anyone in, either. You spend your life away from the family and clan who love you."

"I can't give up my photography."

"I know photography is your passion, and your family would never ask you to give it up. So don't sully your gift by using it as an excuse."

Who was this Fury standing in front of him? "Glad you have it all figured out for me."

"I don't. I just came to earth to have a better life. And I promised myself that if I wanted to live in this world, I wouldn't sit quietly and let things happen to me. Part of that means being honest with those around me. I had to fight to get to this world, so it makes sense that I will fight for what I want as well."

Sergei cleared his throat. "I'm sorry, Lela. But I can't stay."

"You're planning to leave again, right after the wedding and baby, aren't you?" She turned away from him and headed to the door. "Never mind, I already know the answer."

"Please don't say anything to my family."

She stopped, but kept her back to him. "I won't say anything. It's not my story to tell."

Chapter 26

Lela sat in Callie's living room with Kyle and Callie, her sisters. Or at least that's how she had begun to think of them.

Naya walked into the room slowly and sat down in a chair.

"Wow, Naya. You're starting to waddle," Kyle said.

"Did you honestly just say that to me? You know, even though I am eight and a half months pregnant, I can still beat the snot out of you."

"But you have to catch me first," Kyle said with a grin.

Callie held up her hands. "Please don't fight before the wedding. No amount of makeup will cover the bruises."

"What does waddle mean?" Lela asked.

"You know the geese out by the lake?" Kyle said. "It's how they walk."

Lela's mouth fell open. "It's not that bad, Naya."

Kyle laughed. "It's really not. You're one of those pregnant women who look disgustingly perfect."

Callie nodded. "I was big as a house when I was pregnant with the twins. Now *that* was waddling."

Naya looked around the room. "I didn't know what to expect at a bachelorette party, but this wasn't it. Is there no food? No decorations?"

Kyle frowned. "Don't worry so much. I warned Callie that she should not put me in charge of the bachelorette party, so I called in the troops to help."

"We're here!" a voice cried out from the front door.

Kyle stood and rushed to the front door. Moments later, Sabrina and Talia trooped in bearing trays of food with various bags hanging from their wrists.

"Are any of you going to help, or are you going to just sit there staring?" Sabrina asked.

Kyle and Lela went to help them after telling Naya and Callie to stay right where they were. Lela and Sabrina carried all the supplies into the kitchen, while Talia and Kyle went into the dining room to arrange the food table for the guests who would be arriving soon.

Lela listened to the laughing women in the other room with a bit of melancholy. She should be enjoying herself, but the past few weeks without Sergei had been hard. She was strong in front of Sergei, but fell apart on her own afterward. Then she immersed herself in her job with the Bureau of Immigration, and making plans for Callie's wedding, so she didn't have to think about him. But there was no avoiding her thoughts now, since he was scheduled to arrive home today.

"Are you okay?" Sabrina asked.

"I'm fine. The party tonight will be fun for Callie."

"Yes. We're going to have some good food and some silly banter before we call it a night. Callie isn't one to party all night long. Why don't you go sit with Callie and Naya?"

Lela smiled. "I'd rather help you in the kitchen."

"Fine, hide out in here, but only for a few minutes."

Sabrina knew her too well.

"Sergei arrived about an hour ago. Talia said Jean Luc was picking him up at the airport and bringing him back to Aleksei's for the bachelor party."

"I'm glad he's here to celebrate the wedding. His family would have been upset if he missed it."

"His family isn't the only one who would have been upset."

Lela pulled the coverings off of the food trays. "*Sabrina.*"

"*Lela.* I think we should talk about this. You keep avoiding my questions whenever I bring Sergei up."

"And yet you haven't figured out from my avoidance that I don't want to talk about him."

Sabrina frowned. "You're adapting to earth customs too quickly. Earthers, as you call them, have a tendency to hide their feelings instead of speaking their mind. That's not the female I met in the realm."

"Fine. You want to hear the truth? Before Sergei left, he said we couldn't be together because he didn't want to use me like everyone else had over the years. He was afraid he would ask me to give him my powers, so he used that as his excuse to leave me and his family again."

"And what are you going to do about it?"

Lela paused. What *was* she going to do about it? "I'm going to tell him I don't accept his decision. That we can figure everything out, as long as we do it together."

"Damn straight," a voice said behind her.

Lela turned to see Kyle and Talia eavesdropping in the doorway.

"How long have you been there?"

"Long enough to hear that Sergei needs to be schooled," Kyle said. "Do you want me to beat him up?"

Lela laughed. "Do you think you could?"

Kyle acted like she was really thinking about it before she answered. "I'm highly motivated. But if I can't take him, I think Talia could."

The beautiful vampire nodded. "Most definitely."

"Let's get the drinks out so we can get this party started," Sabrina said.

"Yes, it's Callie's celebration, but that doesn't mean we can't plan another intervention as well," Talia said.

"Plotting takes wine," Kyle chimed in.

"Shouldn't the saying be plotting takes a clear head?" Sabrina asked with a grin.

"Maybe, but when have we ever done things the right way?" Kyle asked.

Lela's hopes expanded. This was what family did for one another. She had to show Sergei what he was missing, for all their sakes.

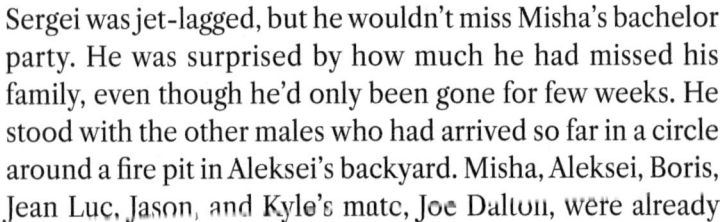

Sergei was jet-lagged, but he wouldn't miss Misha's bachelor party. He was surprised by how much he had missed his family, even though he'd only been gone for few weeks. He stood with the other males who had arrived so far in a circle around a fire pit in Aleksei's backyard. Misha, Aleksei, Boris, Jean Luc, Jason, and Kyle's mate, Joe Dalton, were already having drinks around a massive fire Aleksei had started.

"I wonder what the females are doing now?" Misha asked.

"Probably at a strip club," Sergei said.

Misha and Aleksei choked on their drinks.

Jean Luc chuckled, which surprised Sergei. He'd never seen the vampire show much emotion.

Boris slapped Misha and Aleksei on their backs. "You boys are delightful. Predictable, but delightful."

"Not funny, Sergei," Misha groused. "Wait until you get married someday. I'll remember this."

Misha's words stung. He had never imagined himself settling down with someone until he met Lela. But that wasn't going to happen.

"How was your trip?" Aleksei asked.

"Good. I was in Alaska shooting pictures of the salmon run. It's pretty amazing. They travel to spawn and then die.

Such a powerful instinctive drive, to keep the cycle going over and over again."

"I'm glad they do. I love grilled salmon," Misha said.

Jason laughed. "Leave it to Misha to always bring it around to food."

"Speaking of food," Misha said, while laughter burst out around the fire ring. "What are we having to eat?"

Jean Luc smiled. "The food will be here shortly. I am having your favorite food truck come and prepare what everyone wants."

Misha whooped. "That's the best idea ever!"

Sergei chuckled at Misha's enthusiasm.

"The boys would love this."

Jean Luc smiled again slightly. "Irina is bringing the twins over for a few minutes as well, so they can say they attended your bachelor party and have a snack from the food truck."

"You thought of everything, my friend."

"You asked me to be your best man. That is a serious responsibility."

Misha grinned and pulled Jean Luc into his arms for a bear hug. "I love you, vampire."

Jean Luc mumbled a French curse before Misha let him go.

Sergei and Aleksei laughed.

"What is so funny, my brothers?"

"Nothing." Aleksei grunted as he was the next one to be hauled into Misha's enthusiastic bear hug.

"I'm happy you have found love, Aleksei. You have become a better male."

When Misha turned to give him his hug, Sergei backed away with his hands raised. "I'd like to keep my ribs intact, Misha."

His brother's belly laugh began, and Sergei waited for the bone-crushing hug. Luckily he was saved by the arrival of the food truck. Good thing Misha was easily distracted by food.

Most of the males headed over to the truck except for Aleksei, who stood next to him.

"How has everyone been doing?" Sergei asked.

"If by everyone, you mean Lela, she's doing okay. She's a great asset to the team, and she's been working nonstop to help with training those still in the realm. There has been a great deal of interest in her."

Sergei turned to face him. "What do you mean by interest?"

"Most of the clans have offered to have her stay with them. A few clan leaders have even gone so far as to offer her jobs."

"She's staying with Grandmother."

"Yes, for now. But once her training period is done, she can move anywhere she wants. The other demons who live in the halfway houses will also move on to other clans to make room for the next immigration."

The few sips of beer in Sergei's stomach soured. "They want her for her powers, Aleksei."

"Possibly."

"You have to protect her."

Aleksei frowned. "I plan to protect all the demons from the realm to the best of my ability, but I can't lock her away and keep her from making her own decisions."

It sounded like a good idea to Sergei.

"Since you're back now, it's your turn to keep an eye on her and keep her safe."

Except Sergei only planned to stay until the baby was born before going on his way again. He thought that was the best plan. Had decided it weeks ago.

But his resolution was wavering. Could he keep her safe while staying away from her? Because if he allowed himself to get close to her, he didn't know if he'd be able to leave her again.

CHAPTER 27

The day was sunny and beautiful, so Lela helped the clan set up an outside wedding next to the lake. The past few days had been hectic with last-minute wedding duties. Lela was shocked to learn that Kyle was as clueless as she was when it came to all the traditions, but, according to Sabrina, both she and Kyle went through what she called a crash course in weddings. At least Lela had the excuse of living in another dimension for most of her life.

And speaking of traditions, today the bride and groom and their wedding parties had been separated from each other before the ceremony, which meant Lela had not had an opportunity to talk to Sergei.

But she was okay with that, since the family had planned an intervention for her. A place where she could have Sergei's undivided attention so she could express to him what was in her mind and her heart. If after that he still didn't want to be with her, she would let him go. But not without trying first.

Now she sat in the third row next to Sabrina while they watched the groomsmen escort the guests down the grass aisle.

Besides the entire Shamat clan, there were others in attendance as well. Sabrina was filling her in on who all the guests were.

A handsome man with dark hair and a look of confidence walked down the aisle with a pretty woman next to him.

"That's Griffin, head of the Shifter Nation, and his sister Bea."

Lela blinked. One second she saw a man, the next the outline of a lion. Or at least that's what she remembered a lion looked like from the picture books Sergei gave her. She looked to Griffin's sister, who flashed as a different kind of feline. A tiger?

"Are you okay?" Sabrina asked. "You look a little pale."

"I'm fine," Lela said. "Who's the beautiful woman walking behind them?" The blond had her hair pulled up into a fancy hairstyle and wore a very short dress.

Sabrina grinned. "That's Dolly. She works in the BSR office."

Lela almost gasped out loud at the animal that flashed before her eyes while Dolly passed. She looked away, and caught sight of Kyle's mate, who was standing in the back next to Talia and Jason, another BSR team member. "Joe seems like a nice human."

"He's one of the good guys, and he worships Kyle."

"How did they meet?"

Sabrina rolled her eyes. "That is its own story, and I can't begin to explain it all right now. I'll fill you in later."

Doyle waved to them as he took his seat on the other side of the aisle.

More guests arrived, including a blond man who gave off an energy signal unlike any she had ever seen before.

"Who is that?" Lela whispered.

"That's Nicholas. He runs the BSR."

The music started to play, and Sergei, Aleksei, and Jean Luc walked up to the front to join Misha.

They were wearing what Irina had explained were called tuxedos, and they looked very handsome. Of course, Lela couldn't tear her eyes away from Sergei, who stood at the end of the line. The music changed, and everyone turned to the back, where Kyle stood, looking more nervous than Lela had ever seen her. She wore a pretty, dark green dress and carried a handful of flowers tied together with a ribbon.

But she managed to walk down the aisle, and grinned and gave a very small wave, mostly hidden by her bouquet, when she caught sight of Joe sitting close to the front. She took her position on the left side, and the crowd watched as Callie's friend Jill came down the aisle next.

Then it was Callie's turn. The twins stood on either side, holding her hands. They each wore a mini version of the men's tuxedos, and their chests were puffed out as they marched their mom down the aisle.

Callie looked amazing, her simple white gown fitting her perfectly. She smiled at each of her boys before she looked toward Misha, who blinked back tears.

A tear rolled down Lela's cheek before she could stop it. This family brought out all kinds of emotions in her, especially Sergei.

Boris stood up front, looking very important and serious. The music stopped, and he addressed the twins. "Who presents this woman to be married?"

"We do, Grandpa," the boys hollered.

Boris smiled and gestured for them to take their seats while the crowd tittered over their enthusiasm.

"We are here to celebrate the union of two hearts. I am especially honored to officiate at the ceremony of my eldest son's marriage. This marriage is a commitment, and should not be entered into lightly. Each of you has written vows to commemorate this day. Misha, would you please begin."

Misha held out both his hands, and Callie grasped them.

"Callie, when I first met you, you threatened me with a garden hose. I got to see firsthand what you would do to protect your sons, and I think I fell a little bit in love with you that day. You are beautiful, and brilliant, and you and your boys brought my heart back to life again. I was going to say you're the cherry on top of my ice cream sundae, but you're also the nuts, and whip cream, and sauce. Heck, you're my ice cream sundae come to life. And I will never get enough of you. I love you, Callie."

Callie blinked several times before she was able to speak. "People often say 'I love you,' but they don't really mean it. With you, Misha, love is never a throwaway statement. You love with your whole being, and your heart takes up most of your chest. You honor me by letting me take up residence there. I was afraid to let someone close until I met you. How could I not fall in love with you? When I saw you hug Luke and kiss him on the head when you thought no one was looking, I fell in love with you."

Handkerchiefs were handed around the audience, and tears sopped up, while the bride and groom grinned at each other.

Boris cleared his throat. "Mikhail, do you take Callie to be your lawfully wedded wife, to have and to hold, from this day forward, as long as you both shall live?"

"I do."

"And do you, Calliope, take Mikhail to be your lawfully wedded husband, to have and to hold from this day forward, as long as you both shall live?"

"I do."

"By the powers vested in me by the Demon Council and the State of Ohio, I now pronounce you husband and wife. You may now kiss the bride."

Misha picked Callie off of the ground and kissed her before spinning her around in a circle.

Shouts rang out as people applauded while music played and the joyful couple walked down the aisle.

Lela was so happy for them, but their exit made her stomach jump, since it was time to put the intervention in motion.

"You going to be okay?" Sabrina asked.

"Yes. I have to try."

As the crowd headed toward the community center, Lela slipped away to the rendezvous point. She walked quickly over the grass to a small concrete building that opened to a set of stairs leading down to the compound bunker. Irina had explained that it was there in the event the compound ever came under attack. Misha had suggested it as the perfect place for her and Sergei to meet in uninterrupted private.

According to the plan, Misha and Aleksei would ensure Sergei came to the bunker, and the rest was up to her.

She could do this.

When Lela reached the bottom of the stairs, she halted. She hadn't known what to expect, but it wasn't this. The room was large, with couches and chairs along the walls. An area stocked with water and canned food was in the corner. She peeked into a large closet packed with blankets, towels, and a bunch of other supplies.

Footsteps sounded outside the open door and she turned and held her breath in anticipation of Sergei.

A large male strode into the space and smiled. "There you are."

"Who are you?"

"Someone who's been biding his time all day trying to find you alone, and you just handed yourself to me on a silver platter."

Sergei stood outside with his brothers for a couple of minutes while the crowd settled inside. Kyle and Naya walked up and stood with them.

"Where's Callie?" Misha asked.

"She's freshening up. Irina's helping her," Kyle said.

Aleksei frowned. "You look tired, Naya. You should go sit down."

Naya shook her head as she wrapped her arm around Sergei's. "Are you as overprotective as your brother? Maybe I should have held out for you to come home."

Aleksei growled. "Don't kid about that. I don't want to have to hurt my baby brother."

"What did I do?" Sergei asked.

Misha laughed. "Leave him alone, Aleksei. Sergei has his own problems."

"And what would those be?"

"Do I really need to spell them out for you? Or maybe I do? A four-letter word that begins with an L and ends with an A? Do you truly plan to walk away from her?"

Before Sergei could respond, Lela called out to him. He looked around, but she wasn't anywhere near.

"What's wrong?" Kyle asked.

"I don't know. Did you hear that?"

"Hear what?" Naya asked.

Lela screamed his name, and he stiffened.

"It's Lela. She's in trouble." He tapped his head. "I can hear her."

He closed his eyes. *Lela, where are you?*

He opened his eyes. "She's in the bunkers," Sergei said as he took off running, Aleksei and Misha's footfalls pounding behind him.

CHAPTER 28

Lela stared at the stranger in front of her. He seemed a little familiar...maybe from the council meetings she attended?

"What do you want?"

"Isn't it obvious? I know what you can do. I want more power, and you will give it to me."

She shook her head. "It isn't permanent."

"I know, which is why I'm taking you with me. I'll keep you at my beck and call when I need a pick-me-up."

"No!"

The demon grabbed Lela's arm and yanked her close. "Give me what I want."

Lela glared at his hand as he squeezed her arm roughly. She pushed down the panic that rolled up her spine and looked him in the eye.

She was through with being used.

Lela let the energy she had inside coalesce into a large ball in the middle of her chest. The heat gave her strength for what she was going to do next. She teased him with a small burst of energy.

The bastard actually smiled at her.

And that was when she let her walls tumble down and rammed all of her energy at him.

His eyes widened, and he tried to release her arm, but she wasn't finished with him. He started to shake, and she finally let him go. He stumbled back from her, and would have fallen if he hadn't landed against the wall.

Tremors ran up and down his body. "What did you do to me?"

"I did what you asked me to do. I gave you my energy."

He shook his head as if to clear it and shoved himself away from the wall. "You're going to pay for that."

As he took a step toward her, a shout rang out, and a large body slammed into the male, taking him to the floor.

Sergei!

Sergei reared up and slammed his fist into his face.

Twice.

The male twisted, trying to dislodge Sergei as Misha and Aleksei burst into the room. Misha grabbed Lela and pushed her behind him.

The demon flung his hand up, and an energy burst shot out and slammed into Aleksei, knocking him against the wall.

Sergei punched the demon again, and he collapsed, unconscious.

"Are you okay?" Sergei asked Lela.

"I'm fine. Take care of Aleksei."

Sergei ran over to his brother as Misha made sure the demon was still unconscious.

"How is Aleksei?" Misha asked.

"I'm okay. Just shaken up a bit."

Sergei looked over at her from his crouch next to Aleksei.

"Thank you for saving me. You stopped him, Sergei. Not your powers, *you*."

Before he could respond, Naya came rushing into the bunker, quite fast for a very pregnant female.

"Aleksei!"

"Naya! You shouldn't be here."

"What happened?"

"I got in the way of an energy burst."

"How many times have I told you to duck?" Naya fussed.

"Not often enough, apparently."

"We wanted to make sure everyone was okay," Kyle said.

Misha groaned. "Please tell me you didn't shut the bunker door."

"I did. Why?"

"You told me to find a place Lela could talk to Sergei in private, which is why we chose the bunker. I rigged the door to lock and not open for two hours."

"Well, undo it," Kyle said.

"I could if I could get to the control panel, but it happens to be on the outside."

"Knock the door down."

Misha blew out a hard breath. "This is a bunker, Kyle. The door is made out of reinforced steel, and is several inches thick, as are all the reinforced walls. I can't knock it down."

"What the hell is going on?" Sergei asked. "Why were you rigging doors?"

"We planned an intervention for you," Kyle said.

Sergei's eyes widened as he looked at Lela. "You did this."

"With the help of your family. I wanted to tell you that we're supposed to be together, but now I've ruined Misha and Callie's wedding reception."

Kyle shook her head. "It's my fault."

"Neither of you are at fault," Misha said. "I blame the unconscious demon on the floor over there."

"The demon is Steven Coleman," Aleksei volunteered. "He's the aide to the Haltrap clan leader. He comes to the Council meetings and must have seen Lela there."

"Which means he knows about her powers," Sergei growled.

Misha scowled at the prone demon. "I want him to wake up so I can punch him myself."

"I'm going to punch him anyway," Kyle said.

"He's unconscious. He won't feel it." Misha said.

"But it would make me feel better."

"You are twisted, sister," Aleksei mumbled as he stood up on shaky legs.

Sergei and Naya steadied him.

Misha headed toward the door leading to the stairs. "I'm going to see if I can get the outer door to open. And I'm going to try and use my cell upstairs, although I don't know how much reception I'll get through the doors." His heavy footfalls thudded up the metal stairs. Moments later he yelled back down. "The cell phone doesn't work."

Aleksei bent forward and swore.

"What's wrong?" Sergei asked.

"I don't know. I had a sharp pain in my lower back."

"Are you okay now?"

"It's going away now. Damn, that hurt."

Naya gripped her stomach and grimaced.

Lela went over to see if she could help. "Naya, are you okay?"

Aleksei crowded in front of her. "What's wrong, baby?"

Naya gritted her teeth. "I think I'm in labor."

CHAPTER 29

Sergei swore under his breath. Was this actually happening right now? Or maybe the better question—was his family cursed?

Only his family could stage an intervention that would go this spectacularly wrong. He wanted to grab Lela and figure things out, but it would have to wait.

"No, no, no," Kyle's voice squeaked up an octave. "This is not a good time to have the baby."

"You don't think I know that?" Naya groaned.

Kyle shook her head while backing away, her hands held out. "'I don't know nothin' 'bout birthin' no babies.'"

"Did you really just quote *Gone With the Wind* at a time like this?" Aleksei barked.

"I can barely control my mouth when I'm calm. This is not a calm moment. Lela, have you delivered a baby before?"

"There have been very few births in the realm in decades. I've never assisted before."

"Sergei?"

When the hell would he have ever delivered a baby? "No."

Kyle jogged over to the steps leading to the deck. "Misha! Get down here."

"How is Misha going to help?" Sergei asked.

"He's the only one who's delivered a baby."

"What? When did that happen," Sergei asked.

"Thirty years ago, but I'm sure it's like riding a bike."

Aleksei cursed quite graphically in Russian.

Kyle gaped at him. "I understood that! Shame on you."

"What's wrong, little one?" Misha said as he came down the stairs.

"Naya's in labor."

"Of course she is. Never get trapped with a pregnant female." He went over to Naya. "But we will handle things just fine. How far apart are the contractions?"

"They started right after I came in."

Misha pursed his lips. "Have you been having any minor cramps or back pains?"

Naya sighed. "Yes, since early this morning."

Aleksei did some sighing of his own. "You should have said something."

"I didn't know I was in labor, and besides, I wasn't about to miss the wedding."

Misha interrupted the debate. "Let's get you settled on the couch. Kyle and Lela, grab some blankets and towels from the storage closet. Sergei, get a chair and put it next to the couch so Aleksei can sit on it before he falls down. Then find something to tie up Steve."

Everyone got situated while Misha jogged back up the stairs again. When he came down a few minutes later, he grinned. "I got cell reception. Jean Luc is on the way to get us out, but it's going to take awhile."

Sergei beckoned for Misha to follow him away from the couch. "Do you really know how to deliver a baby?"

"Yep. Last one I delivered was in an elevator stuck between floors. Piece of cake."

"What's going on with Aleksei?"

Misha watched Aleksei and Naya both grimace through a contraction. "I would say he's having sympathy pains, but I think Naya may be projecting her contractions through her telepathy."

"That is so cool!" Kyle said as she barged in...as usual.

"Kyle—"

"What? You don't think it's about damn time a male felt some pain during childbirth?"

"We need to get her out of here!" Aleksei bellowed.

"Aleksei, don't make me knock you out," Kyle said. "Women have been having babies for millennia."

Sergei rolled his eyes. "Says the woman who quoted *Gone With the Wind* a few moments ago."

"I've calmed down since then. I can't lose it if he's going to lose it."

"Lela, you need to track the time between contractions," Misha said, then directed Kyle to find the emergency medical kit in the storage room.

A few minutes later, both Aleksei and Naya groaned through a contraction and then took a breath.

Naya grasped Aleksei's hand. "Everything is going to be okay."

"But the baby is coming early."

"I'm eight and a half months along. Sabrina told me that the baby is fine to come any time now."

"But I haven't finished putting together the crib yet. And we haven't decided on a name. I wanted everything to be perfect."

Naya rested her hand against his cheek. "Don't you start micromanaging things again, Aleksei. Our baby is on her own timetable."

Aleksei kissed her palm, and Sergei was shocked to see the tenderness on his brother's face.

"Don't I know how plans can get messed up. I was going to ask you to marry me tonight, after the wedding. I had the whole thing planned out. It was going to be romantic. I researched proposals on the internet."

"I don't need grand gestures, Aleksei. I just need you."

Aleksei took both her hands in his own. "I love you and want to be your mate. I wish I had done this sooner, but I didn't want to scare you with how fast things are moving. Will you marry me and make me the happiest demon on earth?"

Naya blinked twice before a smile broke out on her face. "I love you too, Aleksei. I will be honored to marry you."

He kissed her forehead. "I'm sorry this isn't going the right way, baby."

"It's perfect."

"Ah, guys," Kyle said. "I might have a solution. I could marry you."

"Are you kidding?" Aleksei asked.

"No. I kind of went ahead and applied for a license on the internet to perform wedding ceremonies, since Misha said I was Boris's backup for his wedding. What if Boris had choked at the ceremony? I could have stepped right in. Or if that didn't happen, I thought I could eventually convince Jean Luc and Talia to finally tie the knot, and I could officiate."

Sergei watched with amusement at the shocked expression on Aleksei's face.

"What do you think?" Kyle asked.

Aleksei shook his head. "I don't—"

Naya groaned. "I think my water broke."

Aleksei turned to Kyle. "Okay, let's do this."

Kyle perked up. "Really?"

"Really."

"Aleksei and Naya's contractions are coming six minutes apart," Misha said. "Let's plan for Kyle to do the ceremony right after the two of them have their next contraction. In the meantime, I'm going to spend a couple of minutes working on how to get us out of here. Hopefully Jean Luc is here by now, working on the lock. Call me back down for the wedding ceremony."

Sergei bit his lip to stop the laughter hovering on the edges of his mind. After years of being away, he had finally come home to find that his family had gone to the demon realm to save his brother. Now he was trapped in a bunker with a female in labor and his panicky brother, while his adoptive sister was going to officiate their wedding. He looked over at Lela, who had a big grin on her face.

Oh yeah, and he couldn't forget the female he'd fallen in love with.

The humor left him. Holy Fates. He almost lost her tonight. And he walked away from her weeks ago instead of staying so they could figure things out together. And now they were all trapped in here because of an intervention his family had planned for *him*.

Both Naya and Aleksei grimaced. "Another contraction," Lela called out.

Misha jogged into the room. "Okay, breathe through it. Good. If I were you, Kyle, I would start talking. Fast."

Kyle cleared her throat. "Marriage is a serious thing, not to be taken lightly. It is an expression of commitment and love. It's not about the obeying crap they used to spout, but it is a partnership based on a willingness on both your parts to listen and compromise at times."

Kyle looked like she was just warming up to her subject until Misha cleared his throat and made a hurry up gesture.

"Do you, Aleksei, take Naya, this wonderful, smart, powerful female to be your wife?"

Aleksei blinked. "I do. You and this child are my world."

"Do you, Naya, take Aleksei, this stubborn, honorable, and loving male to be your wedded husband?"

"I do. Thank you for loving me as I am."

"How could I not?"

Aleksei leaned down and pressed his lips to Naya's.

"Hey!" Kyle said. "I didn't say you could kiss the bride."

Aleksei kissed Naya harder.

Kyle rolled her eyes. "By the power vested in me by the state of Ohio and the wonder of the internet, I now pronounce you husband and wife. You can keep kissing your bride."

Kyle, Lela, Misha and Sergei clapped as the couple continued kissing until another contraction hit.

"That was three minutes," Lela said.

"I need to push," Naya said.

Misha nodded. "Okay. Time for me to get in place to catch my beautiful niece. I'm going to take a look to see how things are progressing." Misha lifted the sheet. "I can see the head! Dark hair like her momma. Aleksei, why don't you sit behind Naya and help prop her up?

"Kyle, get some more towels out of the closet and dampen a couple of them. Lela, get ready to help me clean off the baby, and then we're going to put her right on Naya's chest."

Lela nodded even though she looked a little pale and shaky. Sergei knew how she felt.

Misha smiled. "Everything looks good, Naya. Keep pushing."

Aleksei kissed her on the top of her head. "You're doing great, baby. I'm so proud of you."

Naya gritted her teeth and pushed through the contraction. Sergei wanted to help her so badly, but he was helpless. He couldn't imagine how Aleksei was feeling right now.

Kyle stood next to Sergei, praying quietly.

He looked over at her, one eyebrow raised, and she whispered. "With this family, it doesn't hurt to ask for help from the big gal upstairs."

He shook his head at her with a sigh. "I never thought I would want a sister."

"I kind of grow on people. When we get done birthing babies and escape this bunker, you *are* going to fix things with Lela, right?"

He looked over at Lela, who was kneeling by Misha with the towels in her hands. "Yes."

"Thank God. I told Lela I'd beat you up if you didn't see reason."

Naya groaned, and Sergei's gaze snapped back to her.

"Time to push again, Naya. You can do it," Misha said calmly.

Naya pushed for several minutes, and Sergei found himself leaning forward, as if willing the baby to come out. He noticed Kyle was doing the same thing.

"A big push this time, Naya."

Aleksei held onto Naya's shoulders and murmured in her ear.

"The head is out! Another push and we should be able to get the shoulder out. Be ready, Lela."

Lela nodded, a look of determination on her face. Sergei was so proud of her as well.

Naya bore down again and then groaned.

"That's it." Misha said as he picked the baby up. "Wipe her face with the damp washcloth."

While Lela wiped the baby's face, a small cry sounded. Everyone let out the collective breath they'd been holding. Lela wiped her off quickly while she cried, and then wrapped her in a towel so Misha set her on Naya's chest. The baby settled down once Naya rested her hand on her back.

"We'll let Sabrina do the honors of cutting the cord once we get out of here. Hopefully Jean Luc will get that door open soon."

"She's beautiful, Naya," Kyle said, as a tear ran down her cheek.

Sergei tried to collect himself, but made the mistake of glancing at his brother, who was weeping unashamedly as he gazed down at his wife and baby.

Sergei felt a tear roll down his own cheek as he caught Lela's gaze. Her face had tracks of tears as well.

"Of course she's beautiful. She looks like her mother," Aleksei said in a gravelly voice. "I love you, Naya. Thank you for giving me the best gift ever."

Naya beamed up at him.

A click sounded as the bunker door opened and voices streamed down the stairs.

"They always show up after I've done all the work," Misha said, grinning at everyone.

Jean Luc came into the room, followed by Sabrina lugging her medical bag.

"Dang. I'm too late for the fun part." She kneeled down and performed a quick check of the baby. "She looks good, Naya. We're going to leave everything the way it is until we get you to the infirmary."

Sergei looked over at Lela. He had a lot to make up for. As soon as he could get her alone, he was going to make things right again.

CHAPTER 30

Sergei smiled at the twins as they jumped up and down at the end of the hospital bed. They were just a little excited about having a new cousin. In fact, the entire family was crammed in the room. Sabrina said they could stay for ten minutes, and then everyone needed to get out and leave the new family alone for the night.

Naya laughed at the bouncing twins. "I know you were both hoping for a boy cousin."

"We wanted to name him Bruce Wayne or Clark Kent," Matty said. "But we like her, too."

"Do you have a name picked out for her yet?" Irina asked.

Aleksei shook his head. "We haven't come to a decision."

The twins stopped bouncing and looked at each other. "How about Kara?" they said together.

"Where did you boys get that name?" Boris asked.

"That's Supergirl's name," Luke said.

"Awesome," Kyle blurted. "Supergirl is a symbol of honor and power for women."

Naya looked down at the baby. "I think it's perfect. Aleksei?"

He rested his fingers on the baby's head. "I agree, perfect. How could she not be powerful with you as her mother?"

The boys started bouncing again when they realized they had named the baby. Sabrina shooed them out of the room, rolling her eyes at the uproar as the family said their goodbyes. The boys went ahead of the rest with Irina, but not before they both hollered something about wanting to see Naya's belly later.

"What was that about?" Callie asked.

"I might know." Kyle sighed. "Earlier the boys asked me how the baby came out of Naya's stomach."

"What did you say?" Misha asked.

"Through a zipper."

"Kyle—"

"I panicked! I know I'm their aunt now, but where in the aunt handbook does it say I'm supposed to explain child-birth to seven-year-olds?"

"There isn't an aunt handbook."

Kyle scowled. "There should be one."

Callie laughed. "I'll talk to the boys. They saw kittens being born a few weeks ago, so I think I can explain it without scaring them too much."

Misha wrapped his arm around Callie's shoulders. "The guests are all gone?"

"Yes. Once you phoned Jean Luc, and we knew you were all right, Irina made sure everyone ate and then sent them home."

Misha sighed. "I was so looking forward to that meal."

Callie bumped him with her shoulder. "You're in luck. There's enough food left for us to sit down and eat."

"Really? Well, then what are we waiting for?"

They trooped out of the infirmary toward the community center. Sergei wanted to speak with Lela alone, but the boys had grabbed her hands and were pulling her along with them.

When they arrived at the center, most of the tables had been put away, but a long table remained in the center of the room. A short male walked into the room from the door leading to the kitchen.

"I'm glad you're finally here! We'll serve you now."

Misha grabbed the male by the shoulders and gave him a hug. "Thanks, Tony. You're the best."

The male chuckled. "I saved the meatballs and lasagna just for you."

Misha groaned, and everyone else laughed as they took their seats. Servers carried mountains of Italian food to the table, and the group dug in. Sergei had almost had to fight the twins so that he could sit next to Lela, but Callie called them over to where she and Misha sat at the head of the table.

A few minutes into the meal, Sabrina joined them.

"Baby and Mom are doing fine," she announced.

"What about Dad?" Misha asked.

"He's a little shaky, but he'll be fine too."

Sergei leaned closer to Lela and spoke softly to her. "I want to talk to you later."

She stared at him. "To say goodbye? Now the wedding and the baby have been born, you can leave, right?"

The table went quiet, and Sergei glanced up to see everyone staring at him. Damn, they had all been talking a moment ago.

"Leaving? What is she talking about?" Boris asked.

Sergei took a deep breath. It was his mistake, and he needed to own it. "I was going to leave again after the wedding and birth."

"Was? Has something changed?" Irina asked.

"Yeah. I have. Maybe it's me realizing that I can't do this on my own. Plus, with all the trouble this family gets into, someone needs to stick around and keep you in line."

If he was going to do this, he had to put himself out there like his brother had. He cleared his throat and picked up a spoon and dropped it loudly on the dish, the clank echoing in the big room. Kyle winked at him from the other side of the table.

Sergei turned. "I'm sorry, Lela. I should have listened to you. You're right. I was running away from my family and you."

"Why? When we love you?"

"Because I didn't want to face my emotions. It's easier to run. To distance myself so I don't have to face my shortcomings."

"Sergei—"

"Let me finish. I don't mean my lack of powers, I mean my unwillingness to be a part of my family. And about not having enough confidence in who I am, so I avoid any kind of commitments. And I need to change. I need a family."

"I'm glad you've realized that, Sergei," Lela said.

"Wait. I'm not saying this the right way. When I said I need my family, I mean you as well. I want to be a part of your life. Can you forgive me for pushing you away?"

She stared at him for a long, drawn-out moment. "You did think you were protecting me."

"Yes. I never want to take advantage of your powers."

She blew out a harsh breath. "And I've told you that if I give you my powers it is my choice to make. We can figure this out together."

Sergei's heart beat like a bass drum. "Will you give me another chance?"

She frowned, which was not the response he was looking for.

"Sergei, are your fingers smoking?"

He looked down at his hand in shock. Smoke curled up from his fingertips, and his hand started to tingle.

Boris stood up first. "I know what that is. We need to get to the training center. Go, Sergei!"

Sergei stood and rushed out of the room and down the hall to the training center with his father right next to him. A thundering herd of footfalls followed close behind.

Boris directed him over to the fireproof area the clan used for target practice.

"This can't be what I think it is," Sergei said as he flexed his hand.

Boris grinned. "This is exactly how it started for Aleksei before he formed his first fireball. Is your hand tingling?"

"Yes."

"Okay, concentrate on the tingling, and imagine each is a pinprick of light. Let the light collect in the palm of your hand. Imagine you're holding a warm roll in your hand."

Sergei looked down and did what his father said. After a few minutes, a small ball of fire, the size of a golf ball, appeared in his hand. He looked up at his father, who was grinning ear to ear.

"Let it get bigger, Sergei. Good! Now throw it like a baseball at the target."

Sergei let the ball go, and it hit the wall at the end of the tunnel, way off target, but he didn't care. He made a fireball!

Boris clapped him on the shoulder before Sergei turned to look at his wide-eyed family.

"What's going on?"

Sabrina held her hands above his head. "I don't sense anything different in you." She looked at Lela. "What about you?"

Lela shook her head. "No. The energy is still flowing through him. And I haven't given him any of my energy. We haven't even touched since he's been back."

She was right. Something Sergei would need to rectify damn soon.

"Plus, he used telepathy earlier, too, when Lela was in trouble," Misha said.

Sabrina crossed her arms. "So our earlier conclusion that Lela supplied you the powers wasn't correct."

"Then what's happening to me?"

Irina joined the discussion. "Sergei, we're going to figure this out together. So you haven't touched Lela tonight. Who have you touched?"

Sergei frowned. "What?"

"Have you touched Aleksei?"

"Yes, when he got knocked down earlier in the bunker, I checked him over and then held onto him for a while once he got to his feet."

"And a few hours later, you are able to make a fireball. What about the telepathy earlier. Did you touch Naya?"

Sergei thought back. "I don't think so."

"Yes, you did," Kyle said. "She held onto your arm when we were standing outside talking."

"Where are you going with this, Grandmother?"

"Stay with me for a couple more questions. Lela, you released the block, and Sergei's energy started to flow into his brain."

"Yes," she said.

"And then a few hours later you were telepathic. Did you touch Naya before your telepathy started?" Irina asked.

"Misha and Callie made their announcement, and we were all sitting there on the patio. I don't—wait, I helped Naya walk around the house. She held onto my arm."

Irina nodded.

"And Naya touched you in the hospital room when she was trying to sense if you had telepathic energy. That's when your telepathy started the second time," Sabrina said.

Irina giggled. His grandmother had actually giggled.

"What do you know that the rest of us don't, Mother?" Boris asked.

"I think I know what's going on. I think when Lela healed your energy flow, your true powers finally manifested."

Sergei's stomach twisted and he backed away from his family. "Are you telling me I'm stealing powers with my touch?"

"No, darling grandson. You're not stealing energy from others, you're mimicking their powers. Through touch, you're able to sense their powers and replicate them. We would probably have figured this out sooner if you hadn't run away to take pictures instead of facing things."

"What about Lela? I haven't taken her powers."

Sabrina smiled. "Lela has been giving you her energy willingly. But she has the unique ability of blocking others from stealing from her now as well."

Lela held out her hand, and he grasped it. "I think that means we were made for each other."

Sergei swallowed. "Does that mean you're willing to give me another chance?"

"Absolutely," she said. "But you can't make decisions for both of us anymore. We talk it out first." If she was willing to stay by his side, they could figure this out. He pulled her to him and kissed her on the top of the head.

"How can you be so sure what this power is, Grandmother?"

Irina beamed at him. "Because it's an incredibly high-level power to have. There has only been one demon that I am aware of who had this ability in the past. Your great-grandfather."

"Could he control it?"

"Yes. He could decide when he wanted to use it or not. He could also touch someone and almost immediately mimic their powers, but that will have to come with training."

"I should have known you would be the most powerful of the three of us," a voice called out from the door.

Sergei looked over to see Aleksei standing there.

"What are you doing here?"

"Kyle sent me a text with a video of my baby brother throwing a fireball. After Naya and I watched it, she insisted I come find out what the hell is going on. I'm proud of you, powers or not. You know that, right?" Aleksei said.

"We all are, son," his father chimed in.

Sergei nodded as his eyes blurred and he tucked Lela against his chest. "I owe you all an apology for bailing on this family a long time ago."

"You're back now, and that's what matters," Irina said.

"I'm glad you're home, brother, and this has been one heck of a day. I don't know about the rest of you," Misha announced, "but I'm going to go back to the community center to dance with my wife."

Aleksei left them and returned to Naya and Kara while the rest of the group trailed back to the center.

Misha pulled out his cell phone and fiddled with it for a minute before setting it down on the table while the Beatles' "All You Need is Love" played.

He held out his hand to his wife, she moved into his arms, and they began to dance.

Sergei, and their family, and Misha's teammates, circled the couple as they danced their first dance as husband and wife. When they finished, another song started, and couples joined them on the floor including Kyle and her mate, along with Irina and Boris. Jean Luc and Talia joined them a few moments later.

Sergei held out his hand, and Lela moved into his embrace.

"I don't know how to dance," she said.

"Don't worry, I've got you." And he did.

Forever, he hoped.

CHAPTER 31

Lela sat next to Sabrina while the other couples danced. She had noticed that Sabrina had been watching Misha's teammate, Jason, all night long, but hadn't danced with him.

"This has been an exciting evening."

Sabrina laughed. "This is not what normally happens at a wedding on earth, just so you know."

"I figured that out rather quickly. What I can't figure out is why you keep avoiding Jason."

Sabrina's smile slipped. "Jason is half shifter and half human. He's only known for a year about his shifter side, and he hasn't shown any shifter traits. He doesn't even know what his animal is, if he has one."

"He has one."

Sabrina whipped her head toward Lela. "How do you know?"

"With the shifters I met today, I could almost see a separate energy pattern surrounding them in their animal form. Griffin is a large cat. If I remember the animal picture book I studied, he's a lion."

"And Jason?"

Lela opened her mouth, but Sabrina held up her hand. "Wait, don't tell me. I think you need to tell Jason before you tell me. It's his right to know first."

"I can do that. Why aren't you sitting with him?"

"What do you mean?"

"I mean, your face lights up whenever you look over at him. Why are you not making your move, as Kyle would say?"

"I can't be with Jason."

"Why not?"

"He's a shifter. Succubi do not mate with shifters. It's against the rules. His energy is too much of a temptation to me. I don't want to hurt him."

Lela frowned. "I never thought you would be a hypocrite."

Sabrina sat bolt upright, her eyes widening. "Excuse me?"

"You're actually sitting there telling me that you can't be with Jason because of his energy? Did you not just spend months convincing me to take control of my life and my powers? I did, and now I have a purpose, and I have Sergei. Are there any other excuses you have for me?"

Sabrina gaped at her. "No."

"Then let me ask you one thing. Does he make you happy?"

"Yes."

"Then why are you sitting here with me? Find your cute shifter and tell him how you feel. And when he's ready, I'll tell him about his animal."

<hr />

Arms wrapped around Lela, and Sergei kissed her head as they stood in her bedroom. They had said their goodbyes to the family and returned to Irina's house. She was staying with the boys while Misha and Callie spent the night at a hotel, which meant Sergei and Lela would be alone.

"Where did you sneak off to earlier?" she asked.

"It looked like you and Sabrina were having a serious discussion, and I didn't want to interrupt."

She smiled. "I was just giving Sabrina a swift kick in the butt."

Sergei chuckled against her. "You have been hanging around Kyle too much. Aleksei was complaining about the same thing with Naya."

"Well, your *sestra* isn't going anywhere anytime soon."

"In the matter of a few short months I have gained a sister, two sisters-in-law, twin nephews, and a gorgeous new niece."

His smile disappeared.

"What's wrong?"

"I actually have my whole family back. I'm part of something again."

"Yes, you are."

"But none of it would matter without you."

She turned in his arms. "I feel the same way."

He kissed her lightly on the lips, and she relaxed into his embrace. His mouth ran down her neck and he sucked on her collarbone ever so lightly. She shivered at the sensation, and he smiled against her skin.

"You're so sensitive."

"Let's see if I can repay you." She pushed off his tuxedo jacket and then went to work on his shirt buttons. They were small and hard to open, and she growled low until she finally freed him.

She latched on to his nipple with her teeth, giving him a gentle bite. When he groaned, she looked up at him, full of satisfaction.

"You little brat," Sergei whispered as he spun her around and unzipped her dress, letting it fall to the ground.

She turned to face him, and his eyes heated as he looked her up and down. She was wearing the bra and panties Sabrina helped her pick out. They were black and lacy.

"Damn."

"Damn good, or damn bad?"

"Very, very good."

He lifted her up as if she weighed very little and laid her on the bed, then stood beside her and quickly stripped off the rest of his clothing.

She reached in the bedside stand and pulled out the box of condoms Sabrina gave her before their first time, and he winked at her.

He prowled up her body, and she whimpered when his skin touched hers. He helped her remove her sexy underwear until there was nothing between them. Then he did something so amazing with his tongue that she saw stars and bursts of color as she shouted his name.

Before she could come back to earth, he had sheathed himself and was inside her, and they moved together as one. He kissed her hard, and she reveled in the pressure of his mouth and the pressure that built inside her until she was ready to explode. He stiffened above her, and she squeezed her eyes shut and followed him over with a groan.

After a few moments she opened her eyes and gasped. Sergei's eyes were pitch black and his skin was orange and dotted with red markings.

He looked down at his arms. "Holy crap, I turned into a demon."

She giggled. "You certainly did."

His eyebrows shot up on his orange face, which had her giggling even harder. "You find this amusing?"

"I find it wonderful. And it doesn't hurt that your demon side isn't bad to look at."

Sergei nipped at her chin. "Not bad to look at? That's all?"

"Okay, your demon is gorgeous and sexy. Is that what you wanted to hear?"

Sergei tilted his head. "It's a start." He looked at her for a drawn-out moment before his grin faded.

"What's wrong?" Lela asked.

"I used to think that having powers would be the greatest thing to ever happen to me. But I was wrong. So, so wrong. I would give it all up just to be with you."

A tear rolled down her cheek. "I love you, Sergei."

He brushed her tear away. "And I love you."

She leaned up and captured his lips for a quick kiss. "Are you up for another round, demon boy?"

He laughed and rolled over onto his back, pulling her on top of him. "I think I can handle it."

She expanded her energy and changed into her demon form before starting an exploration of *his* demon form.

Afterward they lay wrapped in each other arms for a few minutes before he got up to use the bathroom.

As soon as he crawled back in bed and pulled up the blankets, covering them, she snuggled into his arms.

"We need to talk through some things. About our future."

Lela nodded. "You start."

"I think it would be a good idea to stick close to home for a while until I get a handle on my powers."

"I agree."

"Plus the immigration is important to you, and you've found your calling working on that."

"I have."

"I want to move in together. We'll need to get a place of our own, since living with my father or grandmother is not going to work for long."

Lela snuggled closer. "We do need our own space. Your grandmother mentioned that your father has been keeping a piece of land for you."

Tears gathered in his eyes. "She did, did she?"

"Yes. She asked me to bring it up with you because, she said, you and your father are stubborn males."

"We are. Would you like us to build a home here?"

"Yes."

Sergei's expression turned serious. "I still will have to travel. The difference is that I will always come home. To you."

Lela's heart warmed at his words. "Of course. I would never ask you to give up your photography."

"Would you like to come with me sometimes? I would love to show you the world, to see it through your eyes."

Lela blinked back tears. She had been doing that a lot lately. "I would love to see the world with you, Sergei Chesnokov."

CHAPTER 32

Sergei was going to be in big trouble. He knew it, and yet he couldn't stop himself. He would do anything for Lela. He had enlisted the help of the twins, and that was where the plan might go off the rails.

Misha would forgive him at some point, right?

Lela glanced back at him with dancing eyes as the twins pulled her through Misha's backyard to the neighbor's shed. The door was slightly ajar, and the twins grinned up at her. Luke pushed it open so light shone into the small space. Sitting to one side was a box with a folded blue blanket filling the bottom. A momma cat lay in the center with two kittens—one gray, the other calico—cuddled up with her.

Lela gasped as joy lit up her face. Sergei's heart actually seemed to stop for a moment before starting up again.

"I told you I'd show you a real cat. And these are her kittens."

"They are so cute," she whispered.

Luke and Matty squatted down next to the box.

"They've gotten big, especially the gray one. All he does is eat," Matty said.

Luke petted the kitten's head. "Aunt Kyle said he eats so much his name should be Misha."

Sergei nodded. "I agree."

Lela looked up at Sergei. "Can I touch them?"

"Yes, they're big enough now," Sergei replied.

The calico kitten mewed, and when Lela sat on the floor and ran her fingers gently over the kitten's head, she jumped out of the box and climbed into her lap.

Lela giggled and cuddled the kitten to her chest. She gasped. "It's vibrating."

Sergei laughed. "She's purring because she's happy. Would you like to keep her?"

Lela's eyes widened. "Can I?"

Sergei nodded. "I talked to the owner. They're going to keep the momma, but they need to find homes for the kittens, and they're old enough now to go to a new home."

The boys bolted to their feet and ran for the door, yelling, "Papa! Can we keep the kitten?" before they even made it out of the shed.

And *that* was why he was going to be in trouble.

But when he saw Lela kiss the top of the kitten's head, he knew he'd do anything for her, including facing the wrath of his older brother. Maybe if he helped the twins pick out a different name for the kitten...

Family was about forgiveness and love. And he had that in abundance now.

He sat down next to Lela and wrapped his arm around her shoulders while she played with the kitten. He had finally found his purpose.

And it was a damn fine one.

THANKS!

Thank you for taking the time to read *Demons Are Forever*. *Demons In The Rough* is the next book in the series. It's about Marrick, the honorable demon portal guard and Naya's friend. Come find out what trouble he gets himself into!

I hope you enjoyed Sergei's happy ending and the third book in the Realm Series. Please consider telling your friends about it or posting a short review. Word of mouth is an author's best friend, and much appreciated. Thank you! – AE

If you would like to know when my next books will be released, please check out my website aejonesauthor.com

Please turn the page to find a list of my other books.

Other Books By AE

Mind Sweeper Series
Mind Sweeper
The Fledgling
Shifter Wars
The Pursuit
Sentinel Lost

The Realm Series (Mind Sweeper Spin Off)
Demons Will Be Demons
Demons Are A Girl's Best Friend
Demons Are Forever
Demons In The Rough
Demons Just Want To Have Fun

The Pack Series (Mind Sweeper Spin Off)
Shifter and the Succubus

Paranormal Wedding Planner Series
In Sickness and In Elf
From This Fae Forward
To Have and To Howl
For Better or For Wolf
For Witch or For Poorer
Till Demon Do Us Part

The Sentries Series
Dragon Kissed
Dragon Charmed

ACKNOWLEDGMENTS

To my usual cast of characters...Faith Freewoman, thanks for taking on this trilogy with storylines that cross over! Nothing like making things MORE complicated for you!

Thanks to Amy Atwell for all of her publishing wisdom.

And a special thank you to Sandra Owens, who read Sergei's story and gave me some suggestions on ways to improve it. You even suggested making changes to the previous book to give readers more of a hint of Sergei. I owe you one!

And to my readers—I hope you've had fun with this family. I sure have.

ABOUT THE AUTHOR

Growing up a TV junkie, AE Jones oftentimes rewrote endings of episodes in her head when she didn't like the outcome. She immersed herself in sci-fi and soap operas. But when *Buffy* hit the little screen, she knew her true love was paranormal. Now she spends her nights weaving stories about all variations of supernatural—their angst and their humor. After all, life is about both...whether you sport fangs or not.

AE won the prestigious Golden Heart® Award for her paranormal manuscript, Mind Sweeper, which also was a RITA® finalist for both First Book and Paranormal Romance. AE is also a recipient of the Booksellers' Best Award and is a National Readers' Choice Award Finalist, Holt Award of Merit Finalist and a Daphne du Maurier Finalist.

AE lives in Ohio surrounded by her eclectic family and friends who in no way resemble any characters in her books. *Honest.* Now her two cats are another story altogether.

Learn more about AE and her books on her website aejonesauthor.com